Weekly Reader Children's Book Club presents

RAMSHACKLE ROOST

Jane Flory

RAMSHACKLE
ROOST

Illustrated by Carolyn Croll

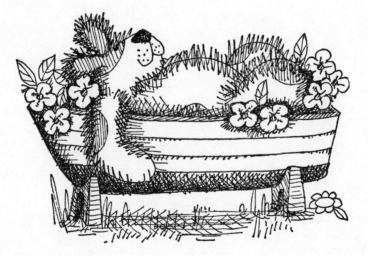

Houghton Mifflin Company Boston 1972

Other books by
JANE FLORY

Clancy's Glorious Fourth
Faraway Dream
Mist on the Mountain
One Hundred and Eight Bells
Peddler's Summer
A Tune for the Towpath

For the real George

RAMSHACKLE
ROOST

Chapter 1

The SECOND WEEK of June 1922 was too early for a heat wave, but early or not, it certainly was scorching. The last few days of school were just a waste of time, the teachers all said. Everyone was too busy thinking about the summer vacation and trying to keep cool.

Now the vacation had started, and as far as the Stuart children were concerned, it was a complete flop. Spring Mount was a miserable town, Cutler Street was a miserable street, and the big old house at 352 Cutler Street was the world's worst place to be.

Hildy and Spence Stuart swung on the creaking upstairs porch swing and quarreled. It was a dismal hot-day kind of quarreling, pointless and rambling. "You did, I didn't, you did so." It was not enough of a fight to relieve their feelings and clear the air, but too much to forgive and forget, so they kept on and on. There was nothing much to do anyway and each one wanted to blame the itchy restless feeling on the other.

Usually they got along pretty well. All the four Stuart children did, but not lately. So many things had happened in the last few months that changed everything. Hildy looked over at Spence, curious to see if he looked any different. No, he looked like the same Spencer Paul Stuart, skinny, tall for twelve, with his knickers too short in the legs, as usual. And his brown hair starting to curl a little because it was so hot and sticky. Wouldn't you just know, she thought, he'd have hair that was easy to curl? Not like Hildy's stubborn straight baby-fine hair that wouldn't stay back with a barrette or ribbon no matter what she did. She brushed away a strand that was sticking damply to her cheek and said crossly, "Why can't we go to camp? Some kids do."

Spence snorted in a superior way. "Camp? You'd be scared. You'd be scared to death of the dark and deep water and snakes and hornets and the other kids. And you'd be homesick. Look how you got homesick right down the block at the Mitchells'. And at camp they'd make you eat tapioca pudding and you'd throw up, and if you had to take archery you'd shoot yourself in the back with an arrow."

Hildy had no answer. It was all too true. Except for the homesickness at the Mitchells'. There was an explanation for that if only anyone would listen. Being away from home hadn't upset her. It was waking up at five in the morning and worrying about breakfast that upset her. What if Mrs. Mitchell fixed soft-boiled eggs? She'd have to be polite and eat them and she couldn't. She just couldn't. She'd be sick. She lay awake worrying for an hour and finally gathered up her belongings, wrote a polite note and crept home in the early dawn, much to the milkman's amazement. And all the jokes she had had to endure ever since had been for nothing, anyway. Mrs. Mitchell had served corn flakes for breakfast.

Spence was still thinking about camp. He went on being logical. "It would cost a fortune to send all four of us to camp. And a fortune is just what we haven't got this summer."

"Everything is what we haven't got this summer. Nothing is what we have plenty of — nothing, nothing, nothing!"

"You didn't carry on like this last summer," Spence said.

"We didn't have the Conrad ladies last summer. Everything turned sour the day they moved in downstairs."

That wasn't quite true. Things had started to turn sour early in the winter, and the coming of the Conrad sisters had been only the finishing touch. The winter months had been full of emergencies and worries and telegrams and bills. To begin with, winter started very early and it was a mean one. The snow would turn to nasty wet slush before they could get their sleds out, and then freeze, making walking a nightmare. The cold wind blew constantly and everyone had a runny nose. The teachers at school remarked that the winter was the worst they could remember, with someone sneezing and blowing and coughing every minute. Then Grandpa Stuart slipped on the ice and broke three ribs and got pneumonia in the bargain. Grandma Stuart was little and frail so someone

3

had to be hired to help with turning him over in bed and carrying trays. By economizing very hard Papa and Mama were able to send them money that was needed.

Then eight-year-old Ellen got a cold and an infected ear, and that turned into hurry-up calls for the doctor and a bill at the drugstore that made Papa gasp.

And before they had recovered from that blow, Grandmother Spencer was taken to the hospital in the middle of the night, desperately sick. Mama, her only child, went out to Chicago to be with her until she was out of danger. They muddled through that, with Hildy and Spence and Papa trying to cook and keep house, and Ellen and Judson trying to help, and Mrs. Smith from downstairs coming in to check on them, and Mrs. Parnelli from next door sending in huge bowls of spaghetti. But the hospital and train fare ate up whatever was left of their savings and no amount of economizing helped.

Papa laid aside the exciting book he was writing about the early days of Spring Mount and the famous Indian Massacre. In his spare time after classes at Spring Mount Business College, he wrote articles and want ads and lost and founds for the Spring Mount *Chronicle*. For weeks the family saw him only briefly at breakfast and seldom at supper. He worked late at the *Chronicle* office and then way into the night correcting stacks of English test papers. But the extra money was needed.

Meals were always nourishing and filling, for Mama knew how to make stew meat and soup bones into suppers that tasted fancy even if they cost very little. Mama pinched pennies until the Indian squealed. All their stockings were darned in the heels over and over again.

Dresses were let down for Hildy and up again for Ellen. Spence outgrew his good school knickers and went right on wearing them with the cuff reaching barely to his knees. Hildy's black serge gym bloomers grew shiny in the seat and the elastic kept breaking, but Mama kept mending it, over and over. Little Jug learned to cut new cardboard to fit school shoes every morning before he left for first grade, and he wore them until the hole in the sole just had to be mended. Mama took clothes apart and remade them, and retrimmed her old hat so it looked almost like new. They managed, and were fairly cheerful about it all.

For Hildy, the hardest things of that hard winter had nothing to do with money. First there was gym. Gymnasium class. Up until fifth grade, they had just played outside at recess time, and that was all the exercise they needed. But in fifth grade they started that hateful, horrible business of gym on Tuesdays and Thursdays.

Fifth grade was a hard year anyway if you were timid and shy, as Hildy was, and inclined to be nervous and drop things. But the gym suit made it worse. A white middy blouse that attracted spots and smears like a magnet, and itchy black pleated wool bloomers. It was hard enough to put up with broomstick drills and Indian clubs when you weren't very good at that kind of thing. But if, in addition to worrying about Right Face! Left Face! you had to clutch at your bloomers for fear the elastic would pop, it was miserable.

Hildy's best friend, Josephine, hated Right Face and Left Face as much as Hildy did, and that was a help. She and Josie felt the same way about a lot of important things like soft-boiled eggs, tapioca pudding and mashed turnips, and the wonderful sad parts of *Little Women* and every bit of *Heidi*. And then Josie moved away. They wrote, but it wasn't the same at all. Sometimes Hildy thought she would never live through the year.

By late spring Mama announced firmly that they were in the clear again, and that come what may, the BOOK — she always spoke of Papa's book as if it were spelled in capital letters — was going to be finished. When Papa protested that he really should teach the summer session at the college, Mama shook her head.

"And let the BOOK wait another year? Nothing doing! The time is now!" she proclaimed dramatically. Mama had a tendency to be dramatic when she was deadly serious. "Right now! You've lived and breathed for the BOOK, and you haven't had a chance to work on it for months. Now is the time, while you are lucky enough to have a publisher who thinks it sounds promising. Besides, if it drags on any longer, I'll be too old to enjoy being married to a famous author."

When Papa looked at their bank book with a worried frown she said, "Stop fussing, Paul. We can manage, you know we can. Everything is cheaper in the summer, no winter coats or colds, and vegetables and fruit don't cost so much. We won't have to spend a penny on recreation. There's plenty to do right here at home."

Chapter 2

Aɴᴅ so it was decided. But all this was before Mr. Smith downstairs suddenly was transferred to a job in another city. The Conrad sisters, the two old ladies who owned and rented out the big two-family house on Cutler Street, decided to sell their own house over in a neighboring town and move into the empty downstairs apartment. They were elderly ladies, set in their ways, and the decision to move was not an easy one for them. Their doctor had suggested that all those stairs in their own house were too much for them, so the apartment on Cutler Street would be ideal.

But Cutler Street was not at all a stylish address and they were worried that their friends might think it shabby or "common." They made several visits to Spring Mount to study the situation and talk to the neighbors on either side.

"I'm not at all sure how we'll take to living in a house with so many children," Miss Emma Conrad said to Mrs. Parnelli next door. "Not that we don't like children, *some* children, but — well, the noise — "

Miss Emma's voice had carried clearly across the hedge between the two properties. Hildy heard it and wished that Mrs. Parnelli would tell the unvarnished truth and scare the Conrads away. The truth was that the Stuarts were nice people but they certainly were noisy. Mama clashed pans and sang while she was cooking, and they all liked to whistle, and young Jug was never quiet. They all liked noisy word games after supper and yelled whenever they had the right answer. Not to mention all the outside games that called for yelling — Red Rover and I Spy and Kick the Can.

But Mrs. Parnelli liked to sing opera. She wasn't very good but she loved it and sang all the time, so of course she didn't notice a little commotion next door. She told Miss Emma loyally, "You won't find nicer, quieter neighbors anywhere, and the Mister — he's a professor at the college. They're very high class."

Papa wasn't really a full professor yet, but he would be someday. Old Professor Hanley was head of the English Department at Spring Mount College, and as soon as there was an opening he was going to recommend Papa for a promotion.

Mr. Miller, on the other side of the Conrad property, told the ladies, "They're fine people, fine and dandy. And that dog, George, he's a great one. Never saw nothin' like that dog. George can bury a root beer bottle in two seconds flat."

Mr. Miller's recommendation probably didn't count for much with the Conrad ladies. He drove the Coal and Ice wagon and after work he sat on his back steps in his undershirt and drank root beer and he didn't wear his false teeth unless he felt like it.

The Conrads hemmed and hawed and finally decided to move into 352 Cutler Street. And that was when the real trouble began.

Miss Emma Conrad was little and skinny and quick. Quick to complain, quick to catch George doing something he shouldn't, quick to hear Jug or Ellen making too much noise. She had a sharp bossy way about her and seemed to make all the decisions for both sisters.

Miss Ida Conrad was big and slow and didn't have much to say. Hildy sometimes thought she wanted to be nicer, but if she did, Miss Emma didn't give her a chance. She would say, "Nonsense, Ida! Give an inch and people will take a mile." And that would be that. Miss Ida never talked back.

The Stuarts and the Smiths had always shared the small backyard for hanging out clothes and for sandboxes and picnics in the shade of the one spindly tree. But Miss Emma and Miss Ida said the wash must be hung on the upstairs back porch, that the sandbox was untidy and eating outdoors drew flies. They objected to many things: mud pies, hopscotch on the front walk, jacks on the back steps, jumping rope, tag, I Spy, children and dogs in general, and in particular they objected to the Stuart children and the Stuart dog, George.

Hildy thought of all this as she sat in the porch swing

and swung her legs. She looked at George. There he was, a big smelly monster of a dog, panting with the heat and collecting his usual cloud of flies. He grinned up at her and attempted to roll over on his back, offering his paw.

"Your turn," said Hildy.

Spence shook his head. "I shook last time."

"Oh well." Hildy sighed and shook the paw that George was flapping. She wrinkled her nose. "He's smellier than usual. What did he roll in this time?"

"Better we don't know. Hose him off before the Conrad ladies get a whiff!"

"If only he wouldn't try to make friends with them," she said. "If he'd just be cool and distant and keep out of their way."

"No, Old Stupid has to shake hands every time they go in or out. No brains at all."

"He's not really stupid. Papa says he's hosty. He likes to greet people. It's what makes him such a lovely dog."

They looked fondly at the shaggy beast. Their affection for George was the one thing Hildy and Spence could always agree upon. George was part spaniel and part sheep dog. When he had grown to spaniel size, something went wrong and he went on growing. He grew to be a huge beast with shaggy bangs that covered his eyes and a sweet smily expression. He was loud, loud, loud! Louder than little jug-eared Judson, even. He didn't bark *Bow-wow* or *Woof*, but a deep *Rumpf* that made the dishes rattle in the cupboard. He was neither young nor trim nor especially active except when he chased cats. He had never been known to bring a newspaper or fetch a slipper. He buried no bones, only root beer bottles which had to be dug up again and returned to the corner grocery for a penny.

Certainly he was no watchdog. If a burglar had ever tried to get in, George would have shaken hands cordially and then battered down the door to make breaking and entering as easy as possible.

But he was one of the family. Spence couldn't remember what life had been like without George, for the Stuarts got the puppy when Spence was only a year old. He guarded each baby faithfully and waited eagerly for each one to grow old enough to shake hands. In the eyes of the Stuart family George had few faults and if George thought they had faults he never said so. He only grinned his broad doggy grin and shook hands all around. He loved his family and the house they lived in and their neighbors and their milkman and their mailman. Being George, he loved even the Conrad ladies and wanted to be friends.

Spence trailed down the stairs behind Hildy and George and watched as she turned on the hose. The Conrads objected to the children playing with the hose but if they were washing George they made fewer objections.

Hildy's thoughts turned again to the long summer that lay before them. "There's Pitman Pond," she suggested hopefully. "We can spend a lot of time there."

"Only if we can spend a lot of money. It's way too far to walk and trolley fare's a nickel each way. Figure that out for four of us."

Hildy liked Pitman Pond. She was afraid of deep water

and ashamed of being afraid, but in the welter of flailing arms and legs at the crowded pond she felt that no one would notice that a skinny ten-year-old girl was splashing happily on the very edge. Josie had been afraid, too. If she and Josie saw anyone they knew they moved close to any small splasher and pretended to be taking care of him. Last summer Spence had tried to help her get over her fears and had made helpful suggestions. But this year, with Spence feeling so grown-up and superior, he'd probably hold her head underwater. And Josie was gone.

"I hate this whole business," she said miserably. "I wish summer was over, and it's just begun."

"Well, don't holler at me about it. It's not my fault."

"Who's hollering?" shouted Hildy.

"You are, that's who! You act as if — "

"Stop that this minute, both of you!" The screen door banged open and Mama burst out on the upstairs porch. "Quiet this very minute! If I have to come out here once more to stop a fight between you two, there'll be trouble. Come up here!"

Mama kept her voice low, but there was no doubt about it, she was mad. They went upstairs in a hurry.

"I didn't start it — "

"I was just talking and she said I was hollering — "

"You were both hollering," said Mama firmly. "I could hear you both up here in the kitchen. Of all times, when you know the Conrad ladies take a rest after lunch!"

"They're nothing but wicked witches, that's what they are! They decide everything around here — when we can talk, when we can breathe, no more croquet because Miss Emma says it's too hard on the grass, no more — "

"That's enough, Hildy. I agree with you but I don't know what we can do. The Conrads do own the house and they do charge the lowest possible rent for a place this size. Whatever else they are, they aren't money grabbers. It's just that they are old and fussy and don't like children, not just ours, any children. And they don't like George at all."

"The Smiths liked George. If only the Smiths hadn't moved away, if only the Conrads hadn't moved in — "

"Iffing isn't going to do us one bit of good," said Mama. "You might just as well say if only Papa weren't writing a book! But he is, and he's got to take this summer off to do it, and I've heard all the complaining I can take."

There was a crash and a squeal. Mama leaped from her chair and dashed inside. Hildy and Spence felt too discouraged to go in and see what Jug had done this time. They sat in silence, listening to the scolding and Jug's surprisingly deep six-year-old voice defending whatever he had been trying to do. Finally Hildy said timidly, without looking at Spence:

"I won't pick fights with you if you won't start anything with me."

"O.K., I guess. We'll have to make up our minds that it isn't going to be much of a summer. We'll live, but we won't like it."

Papa had good news to tell as the family sat down to supper that night. "I've finished the last of my research in the library," he announced happily. "Tomorrow I'll get going on the last half of the book. If I go like a house afire, I'll have it done by September."

The next few days passed quietly enough. Papa ate

his breakfast early and was busy long before any of the others were even awake. Mama encouraged the children to sleep as late as they could so their noisemaking hours would be as short as possible. They went softly around the house, helping Mama with the housework. Then they got out books or paints or checkers, anything that kept them occupied without disturbing the Conrad ladies.

There were occasional outbreaks, of course. Jug climbed the skinny maple tree in the yard and fell. He wasn't hurt, just scared, but he let everyone up and down the street know about it. Jug was loud. He was much like George; everything he did was carried to extremes. Miss Emma came to the window and frowned when she heard his yells. She did not approve of young Judson Stuart, that was plain.

She would have approved even less if she had known how close her sister came to being shot.

It happened this way. The Conrads were super-perfect housekeepers. They cleaned and straightened and dusted all day long and washed each window once a week. Miss Emma did the inside and Miss Ida sat on the windowsill, feet inside, carefully polishing the glass that was already clear as could be. Miss Ida's bottom was round as a peach basket and it was a target that Jug finally couldn't resist.

He had his peashooter and a handful of dried peas all ready to shoot when Hildy grabbed him. She dragged him around the corner of the house just in time. It would have been a catastrophe and yet — Hildy couldn't blame Jug. It would have been funny. Awful but funny.

Ellen had her troubles, too. She got tired of playing every afternoon at Jennie's house, four blocks away, and brought Jennie and Ruth and Patsy home for a tea party. Miss Emma met them at the front door and said crossly, "Four children and a large dog in the apartment are quite enough, so send your friends home at once, Ellen."

Ellen banged the door and thumped chairs and kicked her old teddy bear, all of which was quite unlike her. Really, if any of the Stuart children could have charmed their landladies it would have been Ellen. She was a pretty, pleasant child, gentle and sweet-tempered. She lived in a nice eight-year-old's world, content with her dolls, where all the things that so troubled Hildy didn't intrude. She was not a bit afraid of spiders or mice or dead birds or deep water or strangers or thunder and lightning or the first day of school or reciting in class. But even Ellen, nice as she was, had no softening effect whatsoever on Miss Emma or Miss Ida.

As the days went by, tempers got shorter and shorter. There was a wrangle going on all the time and sometimes two quarrels were brewing at once. If only Spring Mount had been a big city, there would have been lots of interesting things to do — museums and sightseeing and big stores. Or if it had been a small town, the country would have been nearby, with fields and farms and woods to roam in. But Spring Mount was neither big nor small, and the only places of interest were the Civil War monument and the rock in the square where the Indian Massacre took place. They had seen the cannon and the rock hundreds of times, and that was it. Spring Mount didn't offer much except fun in your own home and the Conrads had just about put an end to that.

When the Conrad ladies first moved in, Mama had been sure that she could handle the situation.

"Charm," she said confidently. "We'll just ooze charm and presents and they'll come to like us in spite of themselves." She baked a magnificent cake, huge and rich and chocolaty, and took it downstairs. A little later she carried it back up again.

"Chocolate gives Miss Emma the hives and Miss Ida indigestion. They say it's pure poison for them."

Poison or not, the Stuarts polished off the cake that evening and decided that the next offering would be light and delicate. The next time they had rice pudding, Mama made two bowls. Now Mama's rice pudding was something special, and people always asked how on earth she made it, so she went to the trouble of copying out the recipe ahead of time so she would be ready when the Conrad ladies asked.

The Stuarts ate that, too. Miss Ida looked as if she would have accepted the pudding, Mama reported, but Miss Emma was very firm. The rice was polished, she explained, and they never, never ate anything but unpolished brown rice. They appreciated the thought, she said, but their health was of great concern to them and they could not accept it.

Mama was discouraged, but in her own way she was as determined as Miss Emma. Her next venture was carefully planned.

"Healthful, nutritious, guaranteed not to give indigestion to a baby," she muttered as she thumbed through her many cookbooks. "Help me think, all of you."

They weren't much help. Hildy found her way to the apple section and suggested Apple Buckle, Apple Pandowdy, Apple Slump. Papa looked up exotic things like Soowar Ka Gosht Vindaloo and Sarson Bhara Kekda and Gajar Halwa, which turned out to be some kind of carrot dessert from India, made with hot peppers. Not suitable at all.

The recipe, when they finally stopped being silly and chose something sensible, was certain to melt the hearts of the sternest landladies. Whole wheat bread, sweetened with honey, with the crisp crust sprinkled with sesame seeds. Two gorgeous loaves, smelling just heavenly. Mama put them in a basket covered with a pretty napkin and started down the stairs.

George leaped after her, and in his enthusiasm lost his footing. He crashed down the stairs, and, unable to stop in time, went right through the screen door without opening it.

"Well, so much for charm and presents," said Mama, as she came back up the stairs with the loaves of bread still in her basket. It just hadn't seemed like the appropriate moment to offer a gift. "We'll have to find some other way to impress them after we mend the hole in the screen."

Chapter 3

THE STUART CHILDREN had never before had trouble in finding something to do. The problem had always been just the opposite. But this summer was different. Hildy thought of other summers when she and Josie had been busy every minute, had never stopped from early morning until the last reluctant good-night under the street light on the corner. She missed Josie more than ever, then. But the Conrads had put a stop to the street games; too much noise, they said. The neighborhood seemed depressingly quiet now.

They all tried to think of indoor things to do. Hildy and Ellen cut out coupons from old magazines and sent away for free samples of things, tiny tubes of toothpaste and cold cream, midget sizes of soap and cereal and cocoa. It was fun until they ran out of penny postcards to paste the coupons on. Then the waiting each day for the mailman made the day longer and drearier than ever.

Hildy had time to write in her neglected diary, but nothing she wrote was very exciting. It was the same dreary thing over and over. She made lists of things she would do if she were very very rich, and lists of things she would like to do when she grew up. But her chances of becoming rich seemed hopeless, and she doubted whether she would live to grow up. She'd probably die of boredom before too long.

Mama spread an especially hard jigsaw puzzle out on the dining room table, and they worked on it when there was nothing else to do, which was most of the time, wrangling as they worked.

"Here's a piece of the barn," said Hildy. "That's all I can find, barn!" Spence took it and looked at it disgustedly.

"Barn? For stupid's sake, Hild, this is the henhouse. Use your eyes, can't you?"

Ellen said, "Henhouse? Here, give it to me! I'm working on the henhouse — " As she reached for the piece she knocked apart the whole section that Spence had so carefully put together. Their voices rose and Mama said hastily, "Ssh, it's only a puzzle!"

Papa opened the door of the bedroom he was using for a workroom, and came out slowly and wearily.

"What is it?" Mama asked, alarmed, as he sat down by the table and began to sort the puzzle pieces.

"Nothing to worry about, Sara. Just that this whole idea was a mistake. I can't work, can't do anything at all. Nothing I write is any good."

"But the first half of the book is great," said Spence.

"We thought we were doing all right," said Hildy miserably. "We've really tried to be quiet."

"That's just it. You've all tried so hard, even Jug. It's pitiful. I hate to see you all creeping around, not having any fun at all, just so we can please the Conrad ladies and keep on living here. If I were teaching summer school as usual, maybe we could afford to send you all to camp."

"Camp?" Hildy was quick to say. "Who wants to go to any old camp? We're happy here, honest. We want you to finish your book."

She thought of all the complaining she had done and the fights she knew she was responsible for. She felt she was getting credit for a lot more nobility than she was entitled to.

Jug added earnestly, "Write your book, Papa. We'll be so good the Conrad ladies will get to like us, even."

"You see?" said Mama. "We're all in this together, and we'll manage fine. Next summer the BOOK will be finished and we'll celebrate. This summer we'll all do what we can to help. We'll grin and bear it."

Papa grinned too. "I guess that tells me off," he said as he stood up. "Back to the salt mines and the next chapter."

They tried especially hard after that. They were all quieter than ever. Voices were hushed, shoes that wanted to clump moved around softly, pots and pans never clashed together. George was kept inside where he couldn't meet the ladies at the foot of the stairs to shake hands. The landladies had nothing whatever to complain about. Even so, Miss Emma and Miss Ida sniffed disapprovingly every time they caught sight of the Stuart children or their dog.

Hildy said resentfully, "You'd think they could smile a

little when we're trying so hard. We've washed poor George until his skin is wearing out, just so he'll smell nice, and he's trying too, you can tell he is. He hardly barks at all, the poor love. They just don't want to like us, no matter what."

"They're old pickles!" said Ellen, and Jug echoed loudly, "Old pickles!" and was promptly shushed.

One afternoon Miss Ida and Miss Emma went out right after their afternoon rest. They were wearing their best hats and dresses and carrying their beaded handbags, a sure sign of a special occasion.

"Good, they're going out to tea," Mama said. "That means they won't be back until late. We'll have the whole lovely afternoon to ourselves. Quick, get out the croquet set! We'll have the wildest game of croquet that has ever been played and work off some of our energy. We'll get it put away before the ladies come home. They'll never know."

They set up the wickets close together because of the small yard, but crooked, so getting around was a real problem. They whooped and hollered and swung and let out all the steam that had been building up for days. Papa looked out when he heard the commotion and laughed as Mama expertly whacked her ball through the middle wicket. Hildy really enjoyed herself since croquet was the one game she played well. Jug stood on his head between shots and Ellen turned cartwheels all over the place. They cheered good shots and booed bad shots, all at the top of their lungs. George didn't know what all the noise was about but he barked. It was wonderful.

Spence and Hildy were both trying to get through the last two wickets and be Poison when Hildy hit Spence's ball.

"Drive it! Drive it!" screamed Ellen as all the others cheered, except Spence, who was groaning. Hildy lined up the balls and put her foot on her yellow one.

"This'll do it," she crowed as she swung her mallet with a mighty heave. "I'll knock him clear to — "

There was another scream then, high-pitched, piercing, louder than any Stuart could possibly have screamed.

"Her ankle," shrieked Miss Emma Conrad. "It's broken — you've broken her ankle — "

Mama and the four children stood motionless for a second, stunned. No one had seen Miss Ida appear so suddenly around the corner of the house. Then Mama recovered a little and went to Miss Ida, almost tripping over George, who was hurrying to shake hands.

"I'm so sorry," Mama gasped. "A dreadful accident — we didn't know you were home — "

"It's very plain that you didn't," Miss Emma said grimly. "You've probably crushed my sister's ankle. Move it, Ida," she commanded.

"I can't!" Miss Ida was still moaning. "Yes, I can, a little. I don't think it's so bad — " She tried to lean her weight on it.

"Let me help you," Mama offered.

"You've done quite enough, Mrs. Stuart. You and your children! Quiet as mice, I believe your husband described them? Perhaps you and your mice and *that dog* — get down, you dreadful beast! — will be happier in some other

house where civilized behavior is not required. Your lease expires in four more weeks, if you'll remember. We'd rather not renew it. My sister and I would prefer that you move."

"Move! Oh no, please, Miss Emma. We — we like it here so much, we really do, and moving would be so costly, and it would interfere with Mr. Stuart's work — "

"A long vacation, then?" suggested Miss Emma. "It's the only way we could consider having you stay on."

"Yes," babbled Mama frantically. "Yes, a long vacation was just what we were hoping to have — a nice long vacation — yes, indeed, we would like to be able to leave soon for a long vacation — "

"Then that's settled." Miss Emma was firm. "If you are not planning to spend all summer here you may keep the apartment during the winter. My sister and I — if her ankle is not permanently injured — are going south very early this fall. Come, Ida. Lean on me."

The Stuarts watched in shocked silence as the Conrad ladies went slowly into the house.

"Mama," whispered Hildy. "What'll we do?"

"I don't know! I was so upset I didn't know what I was saying."

Spence was worried. "Mama, they think we're leaving on a long vacation. How can we?"

Just then Papa came to the window again. "Game over?" he called cheerfully. "It's so quiet out there all of a sudden. Why, what's the matter?"

They hurried to tell him, all talking at once but keeping their voices low.

"It's all my fault," mourned Hildy. "If only I hadn't driven Spence's ball so hard."

"It's my fault, too," said Spence. "I was yelling like an idiot."

"It's my fault for starting such a crazy game in the first place," said Mama. "I must have been out of my mind. But I was so sure they were going to be away for the whole afternoon."

"The ladies had no business wearing their Sunday hats and beaded bags on Tuesday," said Papa.

"I have a beaded bag, too," said Mama mournfully, "but I don't use it to deceive people."

"Well, what's done is done and we won't fret about it. Tomorrow we'll find another place to live."

"It will cost twice as much, and this is a wonderful apartment, so roomy and pleasant, and we've lived here for years, and you'll have to get a summer job to pay for the moving and the extra rent. The BOOK will never get finished, never!" Mama was in tears. Papa fished out his handkerchief and dried her eyes.

"Maybe we can rent a warehouse down by the river for our long summer vacation. We'll enjoy the fragrance of the breeze over the water."

Papa was trying to be funny and cheer Mama up, but no one smiled at his little joke. The river he was talking about was a small sluggish stream that ran through the industrial part of town. Smelly factories and warehouses lined it on both sides, and the scent of the breeze over the water was strong of chemicals and rotted piers and muddy banks.

Mama blew her nose and sniffed a few times, and then

said, "No use crying over spilt milk, I guess. Pick up the croquet set, children, and put it out of sight. I don't think I ever want to see it again."

Everyone else felt the same way.

The next day Mama started house hunting. When she came back in the late afternoon she was tired but hopeful.

"I never looked at so many unsuitable places in my life. Either they're big and light and lovely and fearfully expensive, or they're dark and cramped and smelly and the price we can pay. But don't worry, tomorrow I'll come across something good."

Only she didn't, not tomorrow or the next day or the day after that. By the end of the week even Mama's boundless supply of enthusiasm was beginning to give out.

"I just can't believe it. You'd think a nice reasonable place suitable for four children and a dog was an impossibility. Most of the real estate agents just shrug their shoulders when I tell them what rent we can pay. It's not as if I were looking for a house for twenty people, for heaven's sake!"

"Tomorrow I'll give it a try," said Papa thoughtfully. "Maybe if we go a trifle higher — "

"Maybe, but only a trifle," Mother warned. "We worked out exactly what we can afford. Don't let them stampede you into paying more."

That night Papa worked at his desk for a long time, writing down columns of figures, crossing out here, adding there. When he finally stopped, the wastebasket was full of crumpled paper. He shook his head. "Five dollars more a month at the very most. Not enough to make much difference, I'm afraid."

It didn't make any difference at all.

"Firetraps!" he reported indignantly when he came home the next afternoon. "Firetraps and bug breeders! I didn't find one place that I'd want to move my family into."

The trouble was that except for the problem of the Conrad ladies, the Stuarts were entirely contented on Cutler Street. They could walk the seven blocks to school and take a trolley downtown for serious shopping. Mother could dash around the corner to the little grocery store for the things she was always running out of. Spring Mount College, where Papa taught English Literature, was only a few minutes away, so Cutler Street was handy to everything.

The house had a nice upstairs porch that overlooked the backyard, a cracked sidewalk that was a little bumpy for roller skating but fine for hopscotch. There was a high fence in the back that closed them off from an interesting alley with plenty of cats for George to chase. It was shabby and roomy and comfortable and they liked it. They had lived there so long they couldn't imagine living anywhere else, and now it looked as if there was no place else to go.

"Sara, what will we do?"

Poor Papa, thought Hildy. He was a very good writer but not a very good businessman, and all this worry about houses and money had him looking frazzled. She wished she could help but there just wasn't anything she could do.

A strange expression came over Mama's face.

"What is it?" asked Spence. Mama shook her head and

darted down the hall into the big bedroom. When she raced out again she was all dressed up and waving her purse excitedly.

"I've just had an idea. Keep an eye on the little ones, Spence. Hildy, you start supper if I'm late."

"Supper? It's only morning! Where are you going?" they all wanted to know. She didn't stop to answer, only called over her shoulder as she hurried down the stairs.

"Papa had the answer days ago but we didn't know it. The river!"

They watched in dumbfounded silence as she hurried out of sight. Finally Spence turned to his father. "Do you suppose she's all right?"

"Remorse has overcome her," said Hildy. "She's going down to the river and jump in."

"Not in her best dress, she isn't," said Papa. "I don't know what your mother is up to, but you can bet that the bee in her bonnet has nothing to do with drowning herself."

The rest of the day seemed terribly long. Papa went back to work, but from time to time he wandered out to see if Mama had come back yet. Hildy sat on the porch reading and kept one ear open for the sound of Mama's footsteps on the stairs. Spence sat in the living room and looked out every time a woman's heels went click-clacking past, and then sighed when he saw it wasn't she.

"We'd better think about supper, Hildy," said Papa at last. "It'll give us something to do while we're waiting. I'm wearing out my eyeballs looking down the street."

They found odds and ends in the icebox. It wasn't much like one of Mama's suppers so they kept opening jars and adding things, hoping that Mama would come any minute.

Hildy played a game with the kitchen clock. "When the second hand goes around three times, she'll be here." But the second hand went ticking around and the minute hand clicked off the minutes and nothing happened.

George, who liked his meals on time, began to make little growling noises as he sat by his dish. When that didn't work he started to drool. Spence hurried to feed him, and then they all sat there with only the sounds of George's enthusiastic chomping to break the silence.

They waited a while longer and finally Papa said, "I don't know about the rest of you, but I'm starved. Let's go ahead and eat. We can heat things up for Mama when she comes."

They were almost finished when Jug heard the rattle of the front door. "Here she is!" he yelled, and for once nobody shushed him.

Chapter 4

WHEN MAMA HURRIED in the door they knew that her news was good. She looked tumbled and wind-blown, her hat was on crooked, and her eyes were sparkling with excitement.

"Start packing! We're off on our long vacation!"

There was a wild jumble of questions and answers then, with nobody getting anything straight.

"Where are we going? When? Tell us!"

Papa pounded on the table for quiet. When he could make himself heard he said, "Let Mama tell without any interruptions after she has had something to eat. I'll warm up supper for you, Sara. You must be starved."

Long before she had finished eating, Mama began to tell.

"Well, I've had quite an adventurous day. This is what happened. I was trying and trying to think what to do after I made such a terrible mistake with that croquet game, and then I remembered Papa's little joke about renting a warehouse along the river — well, wheels began to turn in my head. I recalled someone told me that years ago before they started to build up the Silver Lake region with fancy summer homes and the Country Club and everything, it used to be fashionable to spend the summer along the river — oh, not here in town, twenty miles or so north of here where the river is clean and the fishing is good. So I thought that maybe, since it isn't so stylish anymore, we might be able to rent a little place quite cheaply."

Hildy squirmed impatiently. "Well, did you find a place?"

"Wait," said Papa. "This is Mama's story. Let her tell it her own way."

"She's taking an awful long time to get to the point," said Spence. "I can't wait."

"Relax," said Mama. "This story has a happy ending. Anyway, I took the trolley and then changed to the train that runs up that way along the river, and I got off at each stop and inquired. Sure enough, there are lots of those little cottages still there, way up on the bank overlooking the river. The only trouble is, every place is occupied and no one knew of any vacancies. Then we went through a little town called Arborley and there was a real estate office and I dashed off the train and there was this wonderful old man named Jenkins and first he said no, he didn't have anything like that listed and my heart sank, and then he remembered the old Hiram Hansen place and said, well, maybe, oh no, you wouldn't want a place like that, not in a million years. Dirt cheap, of course, but no, you wouldn't like it."

"I'm glad to know this story has a happy ending," said Papa. "Otherwise I couldn't stand the suspense."

Mama talked even faster to speed things up. "I felt the same way. The suspense was terrible. I couldn't seem to get Mr. Jenkins to tell me about the Hansen place, and somehow I had the feeling that it was *it*. Finally he agreed to show it to me, all the time saying that he was wasting his time and mine, I wouldn't like it. I almost went crazy on the way to the house. His nephew drove us out in his Detroit Electric, and I was so anxious I couldn't even enjoy the ride. I couldn't wait — "

"I can sympathize with you," murmured Papa. "I never did like continued stories."

Mama started talking so fast her sentences all ran together.

"The instant I saw it I knew it was for us. It's *huge* — it was once a big summer boardinghouse, with I don't know how many rooms and porches everywhere you look and it's way high on the riverbank with steps that go down to the dock with rowboats and furniture and dishes and even mattresses but I'd feel better if we took our own I can't bear a musty mattress and the place has been shut up for years and a great big kitchen that's just a little bit old-fashioned, Mr. Jenkins says — "

The children were cheering and hugging one another, but Papa began to drag his feet a little.

"Mr. Jenkins *says*? Didn't you see it yourself?"

Mama hesitated. "Well, no, to tell you the truth I didn't go in. By the time we got there it was getting dark under the trees — there's lots of trees — and the windows were boarded up and of course there's no electricity way out there in the country, and Mr. Jenkins forgot his flashlight. I was so excited, I knew I liked it, and I was sure you all would like it so I signed the lease right there in the automobile for fear someone else would beat us to it."

She took a deep breath and leaned back in her chair. Papa looked worried. "Sara, did this wonderful old man happen to say anything about the price?"

"I hope I didn't go wrong — I've wondered about that all the way home. He said he'd have to charge fifty dollars for the summer."

Papa whistled. "That's pretty steep for a house that's been closed up for years. But it's better and cheaper than moving. When do we leave, and how do we get up there with all our stuff?"

"I thought about that too on the way home. What about Mr. Miller? Can we ask him if he could drive us up there in the ice wagon early Sunday morning? That is, if the Ice Company will let him borrow the horse and wagon — "

Papa went at once to ask, and Mr. Miller said sure, he'd be glad to, and so that was that. It was all so exciting and unsettling that Hildy was sure she could never get to sleep, but Mama insisted that they all try, at least.

"Tomorrow is going to be a very busy day. There's a lot to do before we're ready. So into bed, all of you, and no fooling around."

The very next instant, it seemed, it was morning. The Stuart apartment hummed with excitement and no one tried particularly hard to be quiet. Mama went downstairs right after breakfast to tell the news to the Conrad ladies. They were openly overjoyed that the Stuarts would be leaving so soon. At least Miss Emma was. Miss Ida murmured that she would miss all the laughing, but then, she always tried to be more forgiving.

Papa and Spence and Jug went off to the store with a long list of groceries and cleaning supplies. Mama and the girls sorted clothing.

"We'll take one nice outfit each," decided Mama, "so we can look respectable if the need arises, but outside of that, nothing fussy. Middies and bloomers —"

"Not those *bloomers*, Mama! Not those Beastly Bloomers!"

"Bloomers," said Mama firmly. "You'll have outgrown them by fall, and you might as well get the last bit of wear out of them. They'll be fine for — well, hiking, or whatever we'll be doing. So put them in, Hildy."

So the Beastly Bloomers went along, too.

They worked steadily all morning and as soon as a job was finished, Mama crossed it off her list. Hildy was a list-maker, too. She always had the feeling that if she could just organize her problems into neat lists and check them off one by one, everything would be all right. She had made lists for self-improvement many times before, yet she was always hopeful that the new list would do the trick.

Before she had gone to sleep last night, she had hastily written a new one and she took it out now and studied it.

1st day — float for three minutes

2nd — kick, holding on to edge of dock

35

3rd — practice arm motions
4th — put it all together
5th — swim

In just five days she should be swimming.

She had done this last year, and had even practiced breathing under water in the bathroom washbowl, but no matter how carefully she planned it on paper, when she got to Pitman Pond she sank like a terrified stone in the water.

This time was going to be different. With no one around except her own family, no one to laugh at her earnest efforts, surely she would learn to swim at last. The very first day she would duck under bravely and hold her breath and open her eyes. Would there be fish in the river, she wondered suddenly, or water bugs — or water snakes? She folded her swimming list quickly and put it in her pocket.

"Lunch and supper will be odds and ends. We'll finish up all the leftovers," Mama was planning happily. "Breakfast tomorrow will be stand-up style. We'll eat toast and jelly right out of our hands and have only glasses and cups to wash. We can be off in a blaze of glory by eight o'clock."

They packed games for rainy days, and five favorite books apiece. That took longer than packing clothes.

"You see," Hildy explained the difficulty to her father, "we don't want to choose thin little books that we can read in a minute. They have to be fat ones with lots of chapters, books we don't mind reading over and over."

"We're not leaving for Siberia," said Papa. "Who knows, there may even be a library in Arborley. Which reminds me, I'd better return all our library books today before we have to pay any overdue fines."

"Be sure to get a good supply of paper and a couple of typewriter ribbons." Mama poked her head out of the hall closet to call after him. "This is going to be a working vacation for you, remember."

Jug and Ellen did all they could to help but they were in the way more often than not. George, too, was underfoot. In order to celebrate whatever occasion he thought they were celebrating, George had gone out and rolled in *something*. Something that smelled terrible. But Jug and Ellen didn't complain as they hosed him off. All the rest of the family was happy and certainly George had a right to be happy, too.

Papa was whistling as he bounded up the steps.

"I had a lucky encounter," he said cheerfully. "I ran into Professor Hanley at the library and told him what we are up to. He was delighted, and guess what? He wants us to take his grandson Guy along with us. I'm so glad to have a chance to return some of the favors Professor Hanley has done for me."

Hildy dropped the paint box she was packing. Spence stood stock still and listened as Papa went on: "He says Guy didn't get along well at all at camp last year, and he thinks a summer with a nice happy bunch of kids like ours might be just what the boy needs to bring him out of the miseries he's been in ever since his parents were separated."

"Oh no!" said Spence. "Not Guy Hanley! Papa, not Guy Hanley!"

"Why not?" asked Papa. "I thought he'd be company for you — he's twelve, too. What's wrong with him?"

"He's a mess, that's what. If we have to take him, I'd just as soon take the Conrad ladies, too. That mess!"

"Spence, that's no way to talk," said Mama. "What makes you think he's so awful? He seems like a nice boy."

"I'll tell you, Mama," Hildy burst in. "He's stuck-up! He doesn't want to have anything to do with anybody. He's a spoiled bratty rich kid, that's what he is!"

"Oh, Paul, if he's that bad, do you think we should take him?"

"I've really made a mistake, haven't I?" Papa groaned. "I don't want to do anything to spoil our vacation, but Professor Hanley is such a fine person, and he was so pleased when I offered to take Guy. I hate to go back now and tell him the boy isn't acceptable. The child's been shifted around from one parent to another, and now he's been dumped on his grandfather like a package nobody wants."

Mama shifted sides. "Spence and Hildy, if we can help him in any way, maybe set him a good example, shouldn't we try, at least? Isn't that the right thing to do?"

Spence shook his head. "It won't work! Not with that one, it won't work. He's — he's all the pain-in-the-necks in the world rolled into one big pain. He's the kind of kid teachers are crazy about and they say, why can't you other boys behave like that — such a little gentleman, so cultured — Oh tripe! We've spent one year in school together and that's enough. He makes me throw up!"

"Spence, I can't do it. I just can't do it. If you had seen Professor Hanley's face — he's been so troubled about that boy not getting along with other children, and when he thought his grandson was going to have a good happy summer — "

"Oh, he'll have a good time, all right. We won't, that's all. Old Gooey will sport around and tell us how to do everything — "

"Gooey?"

"Yeah, G-U-Y, Gooey. *Guy*, for heaven's sake! Did you ever hear anything so fancy-pantsy?"

Mama bristled. "There's nothing so plain about Spencer or Judson or Hildegarde for that matter. Anyway, whatever his name is, he didn't ask for it."

Spence smiled sweetly. "We fixed him. Some fella in the class thought of calling him Gooey. Boy, does he hate it!"

"Who was the fella? You?"

Spence nodded proudly.

"That does it," said Mama. "We're going to give it a try. Just for a week or so. That much won't kill us. Then if he turns out to be unpleasant we'll tell Professor Hanley honestly that his grandson's visit isn't working out. Fair enough?"

Spence and Hildy nodded reluctantly, and went on packing. All of a sudden the day's excitement had fizzled out to a flat feeling of disappointment. Hildy thought miserably, "Either way I lose. If Guy Hanley acts awful we won't have any fun, and if he does reform and behaves for a change, then it'll be Spence and Guy doing things together and I'll be left out again."

But her disappointment was forgotten the next morning as they rolled out of town in the loaded ice wagon. Mama hadn't felt quite right about moving on Sunday. It didn't seem the proper thing to do, but Sunday was the only day the ice wagon and Mr. Miller were available. Then, too, it didn't seem proper to be dressed in old work clothes on Sunday morning when everyone else was getting dressed up to go to church. She finally worked out a compromise that satisfied her sense of propriety and her good common sense. Work clothes and their best summer hats.

"Our heads are dressed up and our feet are sporty," said Ellen contentedly. It seemed to work out well.

Mr. Miller had no problems with his costume. He started off wearing a shirt because it was Sunday but they had hardly reached the outskirts of Spring Mount when he decided it was too warm and took it off. He slipped his false teeth in his pocket and rode along, as Jug put it, in his gums and his underwear.

Mama and Papa sat with him up front on the seat, and George and the children were packed in the back with mattresses and bundles of bedding and clothing and the wicker basket of lunch and Ellen's dolls. Only two could come on the trip, Hortense and Anna May Bella Marie, but Ellen promised to tell the others all about everything when she got back.

George wanted to stand up and lurch around, but after a while he settled down half on Hildy's lap and half on Jug's and barked while Jug and Ellen sang all the first grade songs they could remember.

The ice wagon horse was sturdy, used to pulling heavy

loads, and he walked along at a good clip. Once out of town they passed pleasant suburban houses, each set neatly on a square of lawn. Then the houses thinned out and the real country began. Woods and farms and meadows with cows grazing peacefully, all pointing in one direction. Occasionally they passed a cluster of stores and houses at a crossroads. Papa checked his map again and Mr. Miller clucked to the horse and turned him off in the direction of Arborley.

"I'm hungry," said Jug. Jug was always hungry, just as he was always loud. "When do we eat?"

"There's a lunch, but if anyone dares to open it before we get there — "

"Not even for just a cooky?"

"Not even for just a crumb." Mama sounded firm, so Jug began to count red barns to keep his mind off his stomach.

Arborley was a pretty, tree-shaded town, only a few minutes long from end to end. They were in and out of it before Hildy could spot a library. But there was a grocery store and a hardware store and what seemed to be an ice-cream parlor. After Arborley the road turned to run along the river. Sometimes the river was hidden by trees and sometimes they could see it down below, sparkling and clear in the sunshine. The cottages on its high banks looked pleasant and comfortable and settled, as if they had been there for years and years. Every house had a mailbox out by the side of the road.

"What's our address?" asked Ellen. "Do we have a street and a number? Will the mailman know how to find us?"

"He'll find us, I guess, but there's no street, it's just a little narrow lane that turns off from the road."

"If we don't have a street we should at least have a name. All these summer houses have names. What shall we call ours?"

"These are terrible names," Spence complained. "Dew Drop Inn! Well, Come Inn! Dun Roamin'! Jolly Times! We'll need something special for a big elegant place like ours."

"Now wait a minute," Mama turned around and said uneasily, "I said it was big, but you mustn't expect anything elegant. It's pretty old and overgrown."

"Oh, Mama, you said it was huge and wonderful and had porches everywhere and a dock and lots of boats — "

"Several boats, Hildy, and I'm not sure how good they'll be. Don't get your hopes up and then feel let down if it isn't all you expected."

Hildy wasn't easily discouraged. "I think it will be just gorgeous, and I think we ought to call it something nice, like End of the Rainbow."

"Wait — slow down here, Mr. Miller. I think our lane is somewhere near — yes, there it is! Turn here!"

The children were breathless with excitement as the wagon turned into a narrow winding road that was almost overgrown with brush.

"Are you sure this is it? There's hardly room to get through."

"Oh, this is it, all right. We go around this turn and then we see the house — " Her voice faded away on a note of dismay as they rounded the turn. Mr. Miller stopped the wagon.

No one said anything at all for a long time while they looked at the old Hiram Hansen place. There just wasn't anything to say. Finally Jug whispered, "It's spooky," and Ellen moved closer to Hildy.

Nothing in Mama's glowing report had prepared them for the big boarded-up hulk that clung to the top of the steep riverbank. The tall trees in the woods all around made a dense shade. There were wings and gables and great wide screened porches and balconies shooting out from every side. The screens were rusted and full of holes, and the whole place had a look of long neglect and decay. It looked like a house where nothing good had happened for a long time.

"Are you sure this is it, Sara? Surely, you've made a mistake — "

"You're right on both counts," said Mama dismally. "This is it, and I've made a mistake. A real one, this time. Oh, Paul" — she turned to Papa, almost in tears — "our precious money gone and no vacation after all!"

Papa was stunned, too, but he rallied quickly. "What do you mean, no vacation? Maybe it doesn't seem as beautiful to you now as it did the other night after dark, but it's a house. We don't have to live in style to have fun. We can rough it."

"We'd better change the name," said Ellen practically. "I don't think End of the Rainbow suits it at all."

"How about Camp Chaos and Confusion?" suggested Papa.

"Or Cockeyed Castle?" asked Mama. She could never stay downhearted for very long. It was Spence who thought of the name that stuck. "Ramshackle Roost."

"Ramshackle Roost it is," said Papa. "Come on, men. Let's open up our prize package and see what we've got. And smile, everybody. Nothing could possibly be as bad as old Ramshackle Roost looks."

Hildy's stomach felt as if it had a rock in it. They could all joke and carry on and pretend it didn't matter if they wanted to, but it mattered something awful. End of the Rainbow had turned out to be End of a Dream.

Chapter 5

THE KEY grated in the lock of the back door. After a little struggle Papa got it open and they all went in. They stood in the center of the largest, dingiest, darkest kitchen anyone could imagine. No one had a comment, funny or otherwise, except George. His deep-chested bark echoed and re-echoed through the empty house.

After a moment Mama said faintly, "At least we'll have plenty of space."

"There'll be light, too, when we get the windows unboarded. I think that's the first thing, don't you?" Papa was trying desperately to sound cheerful.

Mr. Miller shook his head sadly. It was plain he didn't think the old Hiram Hansen place had much to recommend it. But he was a good help. He was the one who hunted through the cupboard drawers until he found a hammer and a couple of big screwdrivers that they could use to pry the boards from the windows.

As more light came into the room, Hildy dared to look around. There was indeed plenty of space; plenty of huge cupboards right up to the high ceiling, a very large table in the center of the room, a very large old-fashioned iron stove, and a very small rusty metal sink under the windows. The air smelled dead and dusty and moldy, and there was another smell, too, sharp and biting to the nostrils.

"Skunk," said Mr. Miller wisely. "Skunk for sure. But he ain't been here for a long time. He'll air out."

"What's this funny thing?" asked Ellen.

"A pump. We'll have to pump water," moaned Mama. "Mr. Jenkins didn't mention that." She jerked the handle up and down but nothing happened. "It needs to be primed," she moaned again.

"Mama, what are we going to do?" For once Jug wasn't laughing.

"I guess we're going to make the best of my bad mistake. What else can we do? Fifty dollars down the drain and we're not even sure the drain works." She leaned against the cupboard with her head in her hands and then straightened quickly. "It's so dusty in here I daren't even collapse. Let's get organized and get to work. Don't just stand there, children, be useful."

"O.K.," said Spence. "How?"

"Unload the wagon, I guess. No, wait. There's no use unloading everything yet. We'll have to get things cleaned up a little. Bring out the big box with the buckets and sponges and soap. But what do we use for water until we get the pump going? Oh, the river."

Spence and Jug unpacked the buckets and started

eagerly for the back door, but Papa stopped them.

"Nobody goes down those steps or out on the dock until I've tested them for safety. We don't want any accidents. That goes for the porches, too. Those floors and railings may be rotted. Everybody stay in the kitchen until we have time to check." George decided this didn't mean him and bounded out to explore.

In a few minutes Papa and Mr. Miller came back with the first buckets of water. They had good news about the steps and the dock. They reported that everything was overgrown but in good shape. No loose or dangerous boards.

"Maybe things are going to get better from here on out," Papa said.

"Couldn't be much worse," Mr. Miller commented, setting down his full pail with a bang. "Only thing worse'd be if the skunk was alive and livin' behind the stove."

Mama checked hurriedly, just to make sure. She breathed a deep sigh of relief, and breathed out again fast. If he wasn't alive, the skunk had still left his mark.

There was a pile of dry kindling in the woodshed off the kitchen and a fire was soon crackling in the stove. Mama opened cupboard doors and exclaimed with mixed delight and despair, "Here's a wonderful old teakettle! Oh heavens, look at all these dishes! And these huge iron skillets, did you ever see anything so big? We can feed an army with no trouble at all. But the dust and the mold — ugh!"

While they were waiting for the teakettle to boil, each one had a suggestion about the things that should be done first. Naturally they were all things that required exploring and Papa said no to that. Mama said no, too, because if they got away she'd never lure them back to work. So she said firmly, "Now settle down, all of you. If we're going to eat, we have to have a place to do it in. First we'll clean out two of these monster cupboards, one for food and one for just the dishes we'll need. And the table has to be scrubbed so we'll have a clean place to stack the dishes after we wash them."

Things were soon going nicely. Spence lifted dishes down from the cupboard, then went for more water; Mama washed, Hildy dried, Ellen piled them on the table. Nobody trusted Jug with dishes, but he couldn't do much damage to the worn floor, so he was set to work scrubbing.

One by one the jobs were done. A cool woodsy breeze blew in the open windows and the musty dead smell was gone. Before long the cupboards were dry enough for clean shelf paper.

"There'll be seven of us altogether when Guy comes, and if we have enough dishes on hand for, say, ten or twelve, that'll take care of any company. The rest of these big sets can be put away over here. We won't need ten huge turkey platters or thirteen pickle dishes."

"Why did they need so many dishes, anyway?" asked Ellen.

Mr. Jenkins had told Mama that the place had been used as a summer boardinghouse, and that when it was new and fashionable, many years before, it had been full of guests from June to September. Then summer boardinghouses went out of style and fewer and fewer people had come, until at last the owner had closed it. For over ten years, it had stood boarded up and empty, until now.

"And now look at it, clean and respectable and useful again, after all these years," said Mama proudly. She was being overoptimistic, as usual, for only the kitchen was clean and respectable. But it did look better. They had washed and dried dishes, unloaded the supplies from the wagon, scrubbed the floor. The tattered green window shades were gone and a shaft of sunlight slanted down through the trees into the newly washed windows. Out of the large number of assorted chairs in the dining room, they had chosen the best and placed them around the table in the kitchen.

"We'll eat our meals here or out on the porch overlooking the river, and use the dining room for a playroom on rainy days. The only thing left to do here is to clean the icebox, and then as far as the kitchen is concerned, we're in business."

"Where will we get ice way out here?"

"Mr. Jenkins said there is an iceman who delivers along this road and he promised to let him know. In the meantime, it'll be sandwiches and milk from home and no complaints."

There were no complaints. They spread a picnic lunch on the big table and looked around contentedly at the sparkling kitchen as they ate.

"Real easy meals, now," cautioned Papa. "This is supposed to be a vacation for the mother, too. Once we get settled, if we all work hard for a few minutes in the mornings and after meals, we can have fun for the rest of the day."

They rested awhile after lunch and then got to work again. The afternoon went more slowly. Hildy's first enthusiasm for cleaning had worn off. She, like everyone else, was genuinely tired. But the house had to be in some kind of order by night so the work went on.

From the porch she could see the river far below, gleaming in the bright sun. She wanted to go down the long flights of steps to the dock to see the boats, to see the river close up. Spence and Jug at least had a chance to splash around a little as they filled the buckets, and George had been in and out of the water several times.

"I'd rather live in the dirt for a while," she complained to her mother. "I don't mind if it's dusty."

"Just ordinary dust wouldn't bother me either," said Mama. "This is so thick it's more like fur, and I don't relish sleeping in a fur-lined bedroom. So keep sweeping. And while we're on the subject, let's choose which bedrooms we want and close up all the rest."

"Bedrooms!" The boys were horrified. "Who wants to sleep in a *bedroom?* We might as well be at home!" Spence added, "I want to put my mattress on the porch and camp out."

"Me too!" said the others. "Let's camp."

"What about rain?" Mama was not so sure it was a good idea.

"Well, what about it?" asked Papa. "It would have to be a really bad storm to blow in under this big porch roof, unless, of course, it leaks. And they can all have bedrooms ready just in case. Goodness knows there are enough of them, and beds too."

So it was arranged. The boys were to sleep on the side

of the porch that ran along the north side of the house, the girls would sleep on the south side, and the front part that overlooked the river would be for sitting. Each chose a bedroom out of the many that lined the upstairs hall. They fixed up another one for Guy Hanley and closed the doors on all the rest.

Guy was to come with his grandfather tomorrow. Spence and Hildy talked about it as they swept out his room and dusted an empty bureau.

"I don't think he'll come," Spence said. "I don't think his grandfather will be able to talk him into it. Or if he does come, when he gets a look at Ramshackle Roost he'll go right home again."

"Anyway, I'm glad he didn't come today. By tomorrow we'll have things all set up and he won't have so much to be snotty about. If he had walked into this mess to-day — boy, we'd never hear the last of it."

They turned for a last look at the bedroom — the ornate, carved bed, a dark carved bureau with a long looking glass, a fancy chair with some kind of stiff prickly upholstery on the seat. It would have been easy to exchange the chair for another more comfortable one from one of the empty bedrooms, but Hildy decided against it. Let him scratch his bottom on the prickly chair or get himself another.

"Spence, it will be all right, don't you think?" Hildy was inclined to be hopeful. "I mean, maybe old Gooey won't be too bad, and the house looks pretty good now that we're getting things organized."

Spence said determinedly, "This is a perfect place, Hild. You wait till you see that river, and the dock is great, and the woods and everything. We're going to have fun this summer and nobody, not Guy Hanley or any other boob, is going to spoil it for us."

Hildy gave a long sigh of relief. If Spence said it was going to be all right, she was sure it really was.

Papa and Mr. Miller had been busy too that afternoon. They mended as many of the screens as they could, using good parts of one screen to patch up holes in the others. Papa announced that everyone would have to go to bed early for there would be no lights. They had forgotten to bring kerosene for the oil lamps.

"We'll all be ready to go to sleep as soon as it gets dark, anyway," said Papa wearily. "I don't know when I've worked so hard. How many pieces of furniture would you say we've moved, Mr. Miller?"

"Thirty-five thousand, give or take a few wicker fern stands."

It might not have been quite thirty-five thousand, but between them they had shifted a good many chairs, tables, sofas, bookcases, magazine racks — enough to make them groan as they thought of it. There was such a clutter of furniture that it was difficult to move around. They decided to use only the most necessary pieces and to put everything else in some of the unused rooms upstairs.

In the middle of the afternoon Mr. Miller decided that he and his horse must start back to town. The horse had been grazing contentedly in the field beyond the woods, and both he and Mr. Miller looked as if they would rather not leave.

"Feel like I'm abandoning a flock of poor little sheep to the wolves," he said. "I don't know how you'll manage here all by yourselves. Afraid the house'll fall down around your ears if it's not propped up."

As he rounded the turn in the lane he was still waving mournfully and shaking his head.

"He's got no faith at all in old Ramshackle Roost," said Papa. "This place has personality, that's what it has. Now, no standing around. Let's get back to work."

So the moving and cleaning went on until finally everything was in order. The huge living room and the front porch looked almost bare when they were cleared of the clutter of furniture. A fire was laid in the fireplace, ready for the first cool evening.

Mama stood on a chair and whacked the dust and cobwebs off the big moosehead that hung crookedly over the fireplace. Even when he was dusted and straightened, he had an odd lopsided grin and a foolish look to the one glass eye that remained.

"I don't know," Mama said. "I don't know if I can stand to have him leering at us with that awful smile. Maybe we'll have to take him down."

Jug objected violently. "You keep telling us looks aren't everything, and you can't tell a book by its cover and stuff like that, and right away you don't like him because he's funny-looking."

"Leave him up," Ellen begged. "We've never ever had a moose in our living room before."

"Him I can do without!" Mama gave him one more whack with her broom. "O.K., Mushmouth, you can stay. But not one word out of you! Whatever you're thinking, keep it to yourself."

George loved Mushmouth. From his first glimpse of

the great horned head, George had evidently taken a liking to the creature. He never passed without a deep friendly *Rumpf!* that set the wicker rockers trembling.

The mattresses were lined up on the side porches and the beds were made. The pump was working and water started flowing in the kitchen, first rusty brown and finally clear and cold. Everything was clean and neat except the Stuarts. They were mussed and dirty and hungry and tired. They all flopped in the swings and chairs on the porch.

"Wouldn't it be nice if a waiter knocked at the door now and wheeled in a cart loaded with steaming platters?" asked Papa dreamily. "I would make him very welcome. I'd say, a little of the pheasant under glass, my good man — "

A loud knock at the back door and a shout interrupted his reverie. He jumped in surprise and said, "The waiter! And just in time, too."

All the children rushed out to see who their first caller might be. George burst out the back door and greeted him enthusiastically. It was the iceman.

"Name's Henry Brown," the caller said cheerfully. "Mr. Jenkins told me you folks was movin' in and would be needin' ice. We don't deliver on Sunday but I brang you a piece from my own icebox to hold you over."

"Whew!" he whistled as Mama opened the door of the wooden icebox. "You'll need an iceberg to keep this filled. But it's strong and heavy, and things'll keep good and cold, don't you worry."

As he was leaving he called back, "Might be a good idea to latch your doors at night, you bein' so far out from any neighbors. I hear tell they had a mess of burglaries in Hilltown just last night. The whole town went to the Church Sociable, the Strawberry Sociable, real good food, y'know. When they got back home, stuffed to the gills, I bet, there was hardly a house wasn't burgled. It's a sin and a shame when honest folks have to lock up against thieves. But likely you'll have no trouble, so don't pay it no mind."

With a happy wave, he was off in his rackety wagon.

"Wasn't that kind of him? Now we're all set," Mama said contentedly. "Ramshackle Roost is ready."

Papa lounged in the doorway. "As I was saying, my good man, I'll have a little more of that pheasant, and — "

"I'll good man you," said Mama. "We'll have to have hot baths before we can even think about supper, and I'm so weak from hunger I'll probably drown in the bathtub."

Papa cleared his throat delicately. "There's a little matter I must discuss with you city-bred folks. Baths at Ramshackle Roost are not as casually tossed off as they might be at home. They are to be dreamed over and planned for as a special occasion."

He explained that the hot-water boiler was wood-fired, a venerable old monster that would take a good-sized pile of kindling just to produce lukewarm water. "So," he finished, "I suggest a cake of soap and a dip in the river instead."

There was a wild scramble for towels and bathing suits. The children raced down the three flights of steps to the dock. Behind them they could hear their parents shouting.

"Go slow, there, no running on the steps, slow down — "
But no one paid much attention until a bellow from Papa
halted them all on the dock. When the puffing parents
had clattered down the steps, Papa said, "Before anyone
goes in, we're going to have a meeting."

There was a loud groan from Spence, but Papa said
seriously, "I mean it. Give me your full attention. A
few minutes now might prevent a tragic accident later.
You kids listen!"

While he was mending screens and moving furniture
Papa had thought over the problems of safety and had
drawn up a few rules, which he would write down and
discuss tomorrow. For tonight, until adults had measured
the depths of the water and located any holes or step-offs or
hidden rocks, no one was to jump off the end of the dock.
They would wade out carefully and splash in the shallow
water. No one was to get up early and go swimming tomorrow, no matter how tempting it seemed, and no *one*
child was ever to go down to the water alone, ever. The
rowboats were forbidden territory until they had been
tested and inspected, and then rules would be made for
their use. "And now," Papa said, "end of lecture, beginning of swim."

The beach was stony, with large flat rocks and shallow
pools in between. Farther out the water flowed with a
strong current, but close in to shore it eddied gently
around the rocks in cool ripples. It felt wonderful.

The sun was low in the sky and the trees on the opposite bank cast their long shadows over the water. Ellen
looked across and shivered a little.

58

"It looks lonesome over there. I like it better on our side."

There seemed to be no houses set among the thickly growing trees on the other side of the river. The bank was low there with tall grasses that grew out into the water. It did look lonesome.

"It's better if there aren't any people living over there. We can make as much noise as we please."

Trust Jug to think about the noise. George was noisy, too. He hadn't waited for the safety lecture. He dashed in and out, barking and splashing and leaping from rock to rock. He had always enjoyed water, and here was all the water in the world gurgling and lapping at the shore. It was plain that he considered Ramshackle Roost nothing short of Doggy Heaven.

Hildy felt happy clear through. This would really be a perfect summer. A wonderful river and a wonderful house.

They played in the water for a long time, and when the "All Out for Supper" call came, it was only empty stomachs that made it seem like a good idea.

Chapter 6

Supper was a hastily thrown together affair that tasted simply heavenly to the starving Roosters. They took their plates out to the front porch and ate as they watched the reflections of the sunset sky in the river.

Hildy drowsed in a rocker and half heard the conversation that drifted around her. Their early rising and the day of hard work and the swim had combined to make her eyes droop. She was too sleepy to look as someone said, "See that lovely pink cloud that looks like a boat. It's turning grayer and grayer — "

When the sun finally went down behind the trees across the river and the sky had lost the last lingering rosy tint, the stars came out.

"It's dark! Don't they turn on the street lights out here?" Jug inquired.

"Dark and quiet," said Mama dreamily. "We city folks

will have to get used to the quiet." She yawned and added, "I have an idea the city folks should think about getting to bed while we are still awake enough to find the way."

"There will be light later on, but not until we get some oil and some more of the screens patched," said Papa. "There's still enough light to see — I say we go to bed."

They stumbled into the living room and up the stairs. Hildy's eyes were accustomed to the darkness now and in the dim light that came in through the front windows she could make out the dark hovering shape that she knew was the moosehead over the fireplace. In the daylight Mushmouth was funny. But at night he was something else again. The great stone fireplace was a blacker hole in the blackness, and the faded sofas huddled in menacing clumps.

Ellen shivered. "It's scary," she whispered, and fumbled for her sister's hand. All at once Hildy felt very grown-up and brave. "It's just scary because we're used to lots of light," she said comfortably. "It's the same old moose we laughed at this afternoon when the sun was shining."

Hildy hurried to change into her nightgown. There was a scurrying and scuttling and stumbling all over the upstairs as drawers were opened and closets were closed. They took hasty turns in the funny old-fashioned bathroom while Mama handed out towels and toothbrush glasses. As fast as they could they hurried down the steps again, the girls to the south side of the porch and the boys to the north.

Mama tucked them in and did a little motherly fussing about whether they had enough blankets and what to do if it rained or they needed anything in the night. Then she and Papa said good night and went upstairs like civilized people to sleep in civilized beds.

George was puzzled about these unorthodox sleeping arrangements. He seemed concerned about the beds right on the floor, and padded back and forth between north and south, licking faces and offering his paw in the darkness. Then he followed Mama and Papa upstairs, stopping occasionally to bark, and came down again when he found that his foolish children were really planning to stay outside after all.

There were a few good-nights called back and forth, some plans made for the next day and a sleepy argument between Jug and Spence, and then quiet. The Ramshackle Roosters were all asleep.

It might have been minutes later that Hildy woke up, or maybe it was hours. She had no way of knowing. She had never in all her life seen such total absolute blackness. There was no moon, the trees obscured any view of the stars. There were none of the comforting street lights that always were reflected into her bedroom at home.

And it was so quiet. Her breathing sounded loud in the quiet, and when she moved slightly the sheets made a whispering sound. She lay rigid, not daring to turn her head even a little to see if Ellen was there on the next mattress. After a long while of lying there rigid, listening to her pulse beat noisily in her ears, she discovered that the quiet was far from silent. There were all sorts of tiny sounds, high-pitched singing and squeaking and creaking and rustling and rattling and splashing. All the noises blended into one unidentifiable hum. It was strange but

not really frightening, and it might even be pleasant, she
thought, if she knew what the secret voices of the woods
and water were. Her tense muscles relaxed a little. She
turned her head cautiously and was able, not to see, but
to sense next to her the huddled bundle that was Ellen.

"Everything's all right," she told herself. "This is how
it is out in the country. Nothing to be afraid of." She
rolled over and settled back to go to sleep again when she
heard a sound that brought her bolt upright with terror.

It was a soft stealthy creeping kind of thing. She
couldn't even be sure she had really heard it at all. She
listened — it was gone — and then it began again. Creep,
creep, a pause, creep, creep, creep. She held her breath,
straining to hear. It was coming closer, or was it? Was

it going the other way, to the north porch where the boys slept on, innocent of the danger? And if it was headed toward the south porch it would reach little Ellen first before it came to Hildy. Was it human? Or some dreadful forest animal? Her heart thumped so wildly that the Thing, whatever it was, could surely hear it.

Creep-creep, creep-creep, creep-creep. It moved steadily, relentlessly, but she could not tell where it was going. And then, just when she was sure her lungs would burst and her heart would thump its way out of her ribs — there was the unmistakable sound of Jug's deep voice humming "On Top of Old Smokey." Jug!

The relief of it left her weak, and it was a minute before she could stop her knees from trembling. Jug! And the stealthy creeping sound was one of the old rockers on the front porch. She rolled silently out of bed and padded around the corner. It was too dark to see, really, but she could tell he was there, rocking and humming, as contented as if it were broad daylight.

"Jug Stuart!" she hissed. "You get yourself right back to bed!"

"Why?" he whispered, not at all startled. Nothing startled Jug, day or night.

When she stopped to think about it, it was a good question. "Well, just don't hum. You'll wake everybody." He stopped humming but went on rocking. The sinister creeping noise now sounded comfortable and homey, and after a moment Hildy sat down next to him and began to rock, too. It seemed like a very nice thing to be doing, rocking quietly and listening to the rustle and chirp and whirr of the night noises. Finally Jug's rocking got slower and slower and he yawned loudly.

"Now I'll go to bed," he said. "I'm getting sleepy." He climbed out of the rocker, hugged her clumsily as he passed, and staggered around the corner to his mattress. As soon as she was sure he was safely in bed she tiptoed back to the south porch. There was only time to think drowsily: Strange sounds aren't strange at all when you know what they are. In the morning I'll put that on my list of Things I Have Learned. She had barely pulled the blanket around her shoulders before she was sound asleep.

The next day was wonderful. Because it was their first breakfast, Mama made it extra special. But at the Rooster Meeting that Papa called to order as soon as the dishes were washed, they decided that from now on things would be different.

"If Mama spends all her time planning and shopping and cooking, she'll have no vacation at all. I suggest we agree on one easy-to-get breakfast and lunch, and eat it every day. That'll simplify things, won't it? We can have our variety at suppertime."

This sounded fair, and after some discussion they voted on fruit and cereal for breakfast, and sandwiches and fruit for lunch. Jug nominated peanut butter and jelly, of course, and finally they all agreed on that, even the grownups. Mama said no one ever really got too old for peanut butter and jelly, not if he lived to be a hundred.

Papa and Spence were to be responsible for chopping

65

firewood for the kitchen stove and the fireplace. Everyone would wash and dry dishes and help prepare meals. Each person would be responsible for his own bed, with Mama acting as supervisor and inspector.

"On washday we'll all help," said Papa. "Mama will decide who's best suited for each job, O.K.?"

Papa had typed up the water rules and tacked them to the porch door. Jug couldn't read very well yet, but he understood, and the older children were to see that every rule was obeyed. Papa looked very stern about this and said that if *anyone* disobeyed the water rules, by even a tiny bit, the river would be out of bounds for *everyone*.

Chores were to be done immediately after breakfast, and only then could play begin. Children could roam anywhere they pleased, but until Mama and Papa had time to explore the woods and the riverbank, they must report where they were planning to go. No one must eat any berries, bark, fruit or mushrooms without first bringing a sample home for approval. Above all, they must use their heads or no one would have any fun at all.

At first it seemed like a lot of rules and restrictions, but when they thought it all over the rules made sense. They had all voted on them and everyone had been free to make suggestions. Rules like that were easy to follow, Hildy decided. It was a lot different from struggling to obey the unreasonable rules the Conrad ladies had laid down.

They whipped through their chores in a few minutes, and then the whole amazing country world was theirs to see and smell and feel and splash in, and for George to roll in. It was a little dazzling — so much to choose from, all at once. The four children stood blinking in the one

66

patch of sunlight outside the kitchen door. Where to start?

Spence said sensibly, "Let's all go everywhere this morning and find out what there is to do. Then next time we'll be able to choose for ourselves. Woods first, we've already seen the water."

They followed his lead as he turned to the right through the trees. At one time there had been a wide cleared path for summer visitors to stroll along, for here and there they could see a brick edging. But it was quite overgrown now. The woods had taken back its path and had turned it over to the squirrels and chipmunks that scurried and scampered and chattered and scolded.

Jug crashed through the bushes, racing ahead with George, who was supremely happy. Ellen stayed close at Spence's heels, just a little fearful. This wild growth of trees and bushes was so different from the orderly well-clipped park in Spring Mount.

"We won't get lost, will we, Spence? You know the way back through the forest, don't you, Spence?" Hildy, too, was glad when he answered confidently, "Sure. The old path is still here if you look for it. See, there's a piece of brick under that bush. And this isn't forest, it's just a little woods."

Reassured, the girls began to trot along the path, pushing aside the overhanging branches and squealing with delight at the squirrels who raced back and forth overhead.

"What are all these trees, Spence? What kinds?"

"Heck, I don't know. That's a maple, I guess — looks like a maple leaf. And that's a — a pine, maybe? Some kind of a Christmas tree, anyway."

Spence didn't seem to mind not knowing, but Hildy did. You read about towering oaks and lofty arching elms, she thought, but how do you know which is which, which ones tower and which ones arch? Some of the leaves were fancy and some were plain, some very dark green and others a lighter color. Funny how you could go all your life not knowing that you didn't know something, and not ever knowing that you wanted to know it, and then all of a sudden wanting to know — she got thoroughly mixed up in her thought and decided to straighten it out later. She would start a list of Things To Find Out About.

Spence was right. It wasn't a forest, just a little woods. The trees grew farther and farther apart and soon stopped altogether. They came out at the edge of a flowery meadow, strewn with big boulders. Clumps of golden blossoms grew waist high, and shorter white flowers — daisies? — grew between and around the clumps. What were the low blue flowers with the grasslike leaves? What were they? Until she could call them by their own names they were like Sleeping Beauty waiting to be awakened. Quickly she added another line to her mental list of Things To Find Out About, and ran on to catch up with the others.

Jug had already climbed up onto one of the big rocks and George was barking wildly, begging for a push so he could climb up, too. It took Spence and Hildy and Ellen shoving from behind and Jug pulling on his collar to get him up, but when they accomplished it, George was delighted.

They all sat and rested from their exertions, looking

out over the field. A little bird swooped and sang. Put birds on the list too, Hildy said to herself.

Someone not too far away was driving a tractor and whistling. The sounds carried clearly in the morning air. In the distance, a horse and wagon clattered by. That must be the road they had been going along before they turned off into their own narrow lane.

"Where are we?" asked Jug, and then answered his own question. "We're on top of Old Smokey." He started to sing his favorite song and broke off to say, "Old Smokey is the highest rock all around and I climbed it first so I own it. But you can sit here, too, Spence. No girls."

"Who wants your Old Smokey? I'll find a mountain of my own," said Ellen. She chose a rock almost as high with one side steep and clifflike, where she could sit with her legs hanging over and gasp and shriek about the long way down — all of five feet. The back of the rock sloped gradually and was easy to climb.

Hildy wandered off, too, and found a rock that suited her exactly. It was low and flat, and when she stretched out on her back the daisies grew higher than her head and she could look up through them at the cloudless sky.

I could stay here forever, she thought contentedly. Day and night, sunshine and shadow, starlight and moonlight—

Spence called, "Come on, everybody. Let's go, if we're going to explore this whole place today."

They followed his lead as he said, "If we cut over in that direction we might come out on the other side of the Roost — and then again we might not. We'll stick to the path until we know our way around." He whistled to George, who had gone lolloping off after a butterfly, and they started back the way they had come. Now that they knew the way it didn't take long to get back to the house, and when they reached it they followed a path that led away to the left of the house. The ground rolled up in a gentle slope, across what once must have been a sweeping lawn and was now a wilderness of grass and flowers. A dozen or so gnarled old trees grew on the hillside.

"Apples!" squealed Hildy. "Lots and lots of apples!" They were still only green little nubs but time would take care of that.

One tree seemed especially made for climbing. It was easy to swing on a low-hanging branch and clamber up the slanted trunk. There, in a crotch high off the ground, some long-ago child had built a tree house. One plank of the floor was all that was left, but it was enough to spark their imaginations.

Jug said in an awed voice, "A tree house! We'll have a tree house! We'll get some boards and fix it up and live there!"

"Later," said Spence. "Come on, we can come back anytime now that we've found the way. I want to explore every inch of our property before Guy Hanley comes tonight. I'm not going to have him finding out anything I don't know about Ramshackle Roost."

Beyond the orchard was a sunny clearing that the woods had only partly taken back for their own. It was a tangle of prickly vines and bushes that reached out to grab and hold tight as the children pushed through.

"Berries!" Hildy discovered suddenly. "These are blackberry bushes. Look, they're loaded and ripe, too."

Jug let out a bellow as his shirt caught on a bush. Without stopping to pry himself loose he pulled off a handful of berries and had them almost to his mouth before Spence's shout stopped him short. Jug did not take kindly to his brother's reminder about the rules, but Spence did not allow him one experimental berry.

"We only think they're blackberries," Spence argued. "We never saw them growing before. Suppose they turned out to be some real poison stuff, and you were already dead before we found out? Papa and Mama would be mad as hops."

Jug was unconvinced, and not until Hildy promised they would take a handful home for approval and come straight back with a pail did he change his mind. They were each picking a handful of the biggest, most perfect berries they could find, when they heard the clang of the brass dinner bell.

All of a sudden the Ramshackle Roosters knew they were starving, stark, raving, cast-away-on-a-desert-island starving. Peanut butter and jelly had never seemed so welcome.

Chapter 7

PROFESSOR HANLEY and his grandson were due to arrive right after supper. Papa had hastily lettered a sign and tied a red rag to it so they wouldn't miss the turn. And Mama said, "Just let's get one thing straight. You are not to call the boy Gooey in front of his grandfather. And you are all to do everything you can to see that he has a good time. Do I make myself clear?"

"We'll kill him with kindness," agreed Spence brightly. "Now that's what I call an attractive idea!"

"Spencer! All of you! *Do I make myself clear?*"

They all nodded solemnly, but Hildy suspected that Spence was crossing his fingers behind his back. She was still hoping that Guy Hanley would refuse to come and then everything would be all right.

The instant the touring car stopped at the back door she knew it wasn't going to be all right. There was Professor Hanley, all smiles and waves, in his high stiff collar and dignified best suit. And there beside him on the front seat was Guy, dressed in a very proper camping outfit. The back seat was filled with pieces of luggage. Guy Hanley had come to stay.

Mama was probably saying to herself, Why he's a very nice-appearing boy, Hildy thought resentfully. Because he did look all right — blond and blue-eyed and almost as tall as Spence — with good manners that he saved for adults. Grownups thought he was just fine. It was only kids who disliked him thoroughly.

Oh well, they were stuck with him for a week because they had promised to give him a chance, but at the end of that week — pow! He was going back home.

While Professor Hanley was being greeted and welcomed, Guy just stood there, stiff as a broom handle, looking indifferent and making no move to be friendly. Finally Papa said, "Why don't you show Guy his room and help him get settled, and then you can take him on the Grand Tour — or part of it, anyway — before it gets too dark to see."

Spence shrugged, reached for one of Guy's suitcases, changed his mind about carrying it and started for the back door. "This way," he said grudgingly. Guy hesitated, picked up the largest of his leather bags and turned to follow him, with the rest of the Stuart children trailing behind with the rest of his luggage.

Only George and Jug were their usual unrestrained selves. George couldn't be unhospitable if he tried, and he wasn't about to try. He had been leaping and baying around Professor Hanley and now hurried to do as much for Guy. Jug ran ahead to hold open the kitchen door.

"It's called Ramshackle Roost," he boomed. "That's the name of the house, and we're all Roosters!"

"This is the kitchen," said Hildy unnecessarily, and then wished that the Grand Tour had started somewhere else. The kitchen was tidy enough, and while it was cheery and bright in the morning sunlight, in the evening none of the last rays of the sun reached it, and it had a gloomy brooding look, shadowy in the dark corners.

And there was that faint, unmistakable smell of skunk. All the scrubbing and cleaning and airing had not been enough to erase it completely. The Roosters had quickly gotten used to it and hardly noticed it, but the smell was still there. Guy sniffed but said nothing. They marched through the almost empty dining room without comment.

"And this is the living room," said Hildy, again unnecessarily. Guy flicked a glance at her and said nothing. No comment on the size of the huge room, or Mushmouth grinning cheerily over the mammoth fireplace. Nothing but that quick scornful glance that said plainly, I can tell it's a living room, stupid, and I'm not impressed.

Hildy felt her cheeks grow hot. Why did she always think she had to say something, even if it was the wrong thing? Put that on your list, she said to herself. Learn to keep your mouth shut.

George liked processions. He leaped ahead of the group and showed them the way upstairs, then rushed back to herd any stragglers, urging them to hurry, stepping on their heels and nuzzling the backs of their knees. The Stuarts should have been used to it, but they still squealed and giggled whenever George's wet nose touched the back of their bare legs. Guy said nothing.

Spence led the way to the bedroom they had made ready for their visitor. They all crowded in and waited for him to say something, anything. Spence opened the heavy carved wardrobe and said, "You can hang your suits in here." There was a mocking edge to his voice and Guy said quickly, "I didn't bring any suits. I didn't expect it to be formal."

Spence laughed, and after a tiny pause, so did everyone else. Nervous uncomfortable laughter, because they didn't know what to say and it seemed to be rude to be just standing there. Hildy made one more attempt at friendly conversation.

"There's a chair — for sitting on — " Oh, for heaven's

sake! He'd think she was a complete idiot! What were chairs for, anyway? "I mean — the chair is prickly — sort of — and if you don't like prickly chairs — " Confused, she let her sentence trail off. What were they to do now? Papa had said, Help Guy get settled. Did he mean they were all to stand around while he unpacked? Just stand there and gawk while he put away his underwear and socks? He had brought quite a lot, even a tennis racket and a bedroll and a volleyball.

George saved the day. He stood up with his great paws on Guy's shoulders and licked the guest's face lovingly. Then he sat down again and lifted his paw to be shaken. It was a genuine welcome, straight from the heart, and everyone laughed. Real laughter this time, no edge of mockery or embarrassment and for the moment it made Guy one of them.

"You can unpack later," Spence said. "You have a balcony all to yourself — all the front bedrooms do."

"And a screen with no holes in it," Jug added eagerly.

"The bed's not too bad. Come on down now and we'll show you the rest."

No mention of the beds on the porch at all. Had Spence forgotten? Or was he not mentioning it on purpose? Hildy was tempted to ask but remembered her new resolution just in time. Without saying a word she turned and followed the others down the stairs.

They paused long enough for Guy to read the water rules tacked to the porch door. He gave a little snort.

"Baby stuff!"

"Papa isn't just kidding," Hildy warned. "Everybody goes by the rules or nobody goes in. He means it."

Guy nodded carelessly, as if rules didn't matter much one way or the other. They clattered down the first flight of steps, across the paved terrace where there had once been a shallow pool or a fountain, and down the last of the steps to the dock. If they had expected Guy to be impressed they were disappointed.

"Too bad it's not a sandy beach. These rocky beaches are a pain. How deep is it at the end of the dock?"

Spence admitted reluctantly that they weren't sure, there hadn't been time to find out exactly. He said defensively, "We've been busy here, you know — there's more to do than just measure water."

Guy nodded carelessly again, and kicked at one of the overturned boats. "Let's get these in the water. We can have races."

Jug spoke up. "Papa'll skin us alive if we go out in the boats before he checks them. They've maybe got holes in them."

"I'll check them out," said Guy. "You know, it's not bad here. A lake's better, of course, but a river is O.K. if you don't have anything better."

There seemed to be no answer to this. The Stuarts hadn't any experience with either lakes or rivers. They all looked out over the sparkling water, darkening now in the twilight. Long shadows reached clear across to the other side. The current ran swiftly out in the center and lapped gently against the big flat rocks near the shore. What could be nicer than this?

"It's just beautiful here!" said Ellen suddenly. "I think it's the prettiest river in the whole world, so there!"

She stuck her tongue out at Guy and marched up the

steps, stamping as she went. Jug followed her. Hildy didn't know whether to go or stay.

"What's she mad about?" asked Guy. "I didn't say anything about her old river." Spence shrugged, and Hildy thought miserably, If this is the way it's going to be, we might as well be home with the Conrad ladies.

It was getting too dark to see much. Spence muttered something about seeing the rest of the place in the morning, and the three of them went back up to join the others on the big front porch.

"It's absolute heaven here," said Mama. "I'm going to rock for days at a time and restore my soul."

"None of that for me," said Papa. "Tomorrow I begin on my writing. I've a room all ready on the back of the house, away from everything. I've moved the bed out and a table in, and the window looks out right into a tree. Nothing to distract me there. I'll be able to get a lot done."

Ellen and Jug were playing tree tag out in the back. They sounded happy, Hildy thought wistfully. If Guy weren't there, she and Spence would have joined them, and it wouldn't matter at all that tree tag was really a little kid's game.

Finally Professor Hanley said he must go, because it was a long ride back to Spring Mount. They all trooped out to say good-bye. George had ventured off into the woods, barking and crashing through the brush as he chased something. But when he heard the sound of the car starting he bounded back in time to say good-bye. George said good-bye in as satisfactory a way as he said hello. You always knew he was sorry to see you go. They all stood there until the taillights of the auto flickered around the bend. They could hear the sound of tires on gravel for a moment or two longer, and then he was gone.

Papa said cheerfully, "Well, now, Guy, I guess you're stuck with us for a while. Think you'll like it?"

"Oh, yes indeed, sir. It's really very nice."

Hildy looked at Spence, but she couldn't see his expression in the dark. She had a good idea what he was thinking.

Mama was already herding the younger children inside. They were reluctant, complaining that it was still early, that they hadn't finished their game, that they weren't tired. Mama was firm. "And it's bedtime for you older ones in a few minutes," she called. "Just as soon as I get these wildcats bedded down."

Somehow in the confusion of getting ready for bed, with the doors banging and all the calling back and forth, Mama didn't notice that Guy wasn't with the others until she made her rounds, tucking in and saying good night. Hildy could hear her voice, "Good-night, Jug. Quiet, now. No talking. Good night, Spence, Guy — Why, where's Guy?"

Spence yawned elaborately, as if he had been almost asleep. "Oh, he's sleeping upstairs. He'll be more comfortable there."

"Oh," said Mama, surprised. "Of course, if that's the way he wants it — " She did not notice, as Hildy did, that Spence hadn't said Guy wanted it that way. He just let her think he had said it.

Hildy had a hard time going to sleep. She heard George pad up and down the steps several times, and finally push open a door upstairs. A bed creaked under his weight. He must have decided to spend the night on someone's bed instead of on the porch floor. She wondered who had been favored with the smelly honor. She'd know in the morning when she saw who was scratching flea bites.

The strange soft noises of the night were more familiar to her now and caused her only a moment's anxiety. The night noises didn't keep her awake. The thing that drove sleep away was a nagging feeling that justice was not being done. Guy was a guest, whether they liked it or not, and you were supposed to be kind to guests. The largest cooky, or the last one if there was only one left, the most comfortable chair, company manners. Mama had drilled this into them all their lives, since they were little kids.

"Let Sonny play with your train — he's your guest. Madeline first, Hildy, she's company. Jug, not the biggest piece — no, Jug! I don't care if you think Edna is a pain in the neck, she's coming to visit and you'll be polite, or else."

It would be Or Else, Hildy reflected grimly, if Papa and Mama found that Spence was freezing Guy Hanley right out. They wouldn't like it one bit. And how long would it take for Guy to notice that the other children were down on the porch, sleeping almost out under the trees, while he was up in a stuffy bedroom with a prickly chair for company?

Her sympathy shifted then, swung right around like a weather vane.

Serves the stuck-up old thing right, she thought. He's probably too fancy-pantsy to sleep on the floor, anyway. He's only going to spoil our fun, making cracks

80

about our gorgeous river, and our perfectly good safety rules —

She listened to the sounds of the gorgeous river that hummed and burbled as the current pushed against rocks and fallen trees. It was like a lullaby, she thought. A baby could listen to that and pretty soon it would close its little eyes — and fall off — to sleep —

Chapter 8

O<small>NCE THE SCREENS</small> were mended and the bushes and vines cleared away from the steps, Papa's next chore was to help Jug with his tree house. There were enough sound boards in the tool shed and it didn't take long to make a broad platform high enough to please Jug and sturdy enough to satisfy Papa. With a row of two-by-twos nailed to the trunk for foot- and handholds and a wooden bucket on a rope for hauling up provisions, it was as complete a tree house as anyone could ask for.

From the very first, Jug claimed it. But he was a generous little boy and allowed any of the others to climb up there too. It was a perfect place for playing and even Mama approved and wasn't worried. It wasn't too far off the ground — Jug would have built it in the very topmost branch of the tree if he had had his way — and the ground beneath it was cushioned with meadow grasses and wild flowers. Ellen put her dolls, Hortense and Anna May Bella Marie, in the bucket and Jug pulled them up. A sturdy tin box with a lid protected his treasures from rain and his snacks from the squirrels. From the deck of the tree house he was able to be captain of a great ocean liner or a whaling vessel, or the helmeted pilot of a flying machine, while Ellen and Hortense and Anna May Bella Marie went along as crew.

Once, when everyone was safely occupied with something else, Hildy tried lying on her stomach with her head and arms extending out over the edge to practice swimming strokes. It worked fine, but she felt silly doing it, and knew she would feel even sillier if someone came along and saw her. Swimming in the air was wonderful and completely safe. Later, the same confident strokes did not work so well in the water. She thrashed around, got water up her nose and in her eyes and gave up again.

She still loved the tree house, even if it did not solve her swimming problem. *Little Women* was twice as interesting, and Jug's shouts to his lookout in the crow's nest were no more disturbing than the twittering of the robins all around her.

Even Spence sometimes went up the tree to lie on his back and look up at the changing pattern of blue sky and green leaves. Guy tried it once or twice, but he always recalled a tree house in his past, a magnificent structure that had everything, it seemed, except running water, and maybe even that. At any rate he was not a comfortable visitor and was not urged to come again.

The other Rooster who was not absolutely delighted with the tree house was George. True, he never stayed in one place long, anyway, and was always dashing away to bark at a rabbit or chase a chipmunk. But then he would dash back again to sit mournfully under the tree. He would look up, hopeful that one of his adored family would ask him to come up. Ellen tried to show him how easy it would be to put his paws on the handholds and climb up, while Jug pushed from behind. But it was not that easy for George and he was far too heavy for a skinny little boy to shove. He was too heavy to lift, too. Jug and Ellen together tried to haul him up in the bucket, but even by pulling as hard as they could, they could not budge George. Jug was sure there was a way and was determined to find it somehow.

One day while sorting through some interesting junk in the tool shed, along with seven bent and rusty nails and a perfectly good pair of pliers, he found a pulley. Spence knew what it was, and as soon as he explained how it worked, ideas began to go off in Jug's head, snapping and popping like firecrackers. He didn't explain his plan to anyone, not even Ellen, but set about making it work. When he had attached the pulley firmly to a limb of the tree, and when further hunting turned up a length of rope, and when he had hammered together a crude platform about two feet square, only then did he confide in Ellen. He needed a helper to work out his plan and Ellen was it.

"See," he explained, "George is on the ground and I'm up here and so are you. George steps on the platform and he sits down or he's liable to fall off. I climb into the bucket up here and I start to go down and that pulls George up. When I get to the ground, George will be up here at the top, you help him off the platform, then I climb up and we're all here."

Ellen was amazed. "For a little kid, you do think up good ideas! Just you wait, lovey," she called down to George who was snuffing unhappily at the foot of the tree. "Jug'll have you up here in a jiffy."

Actually it took considerably longer than a jiffy. There were minor interruptions — George lost interest and went off after a rabbit. Before they could entice him back the dinner bell rang, but finally everything seemed ready. Ellen coaxed George to sit on the rickety platform by sitting down with him and scratching his ears. Before long he was sprawled out, sound asleep and overhanging on all sides. Then as quietly as she could she climbed up the tree to join Jug. He stepped into the bucket and — nothing happened. Nothing at all. George went on dreaming and twitching on the ground and Jug sat there in the bucket high up in the air.

Ellen was so disappointed that she had to swallow hard to keep from crying. Jug was disappointed too, but he kept on trying.

"George is heavier than I am, that's what. The heaviest one has to be in the bucket."

"You'll never get George in there, not even if you stuff him in and lean on him."

"Not George in the bucket. You."

Ellen backed away. "Not me, I'm only eight years old and I'm skinnier'n George and that bucket is splintery. Not me!"

Jug was thinking fast. "If you sat in the bucket and held a brick in your lap to make you weigh more — "

And that is what they did. Jug made several quick trips to the tool shed for a supply of bricks, and then, urging and coaxing and reassuring, helped Ellen into the swaying wooden bucket. She crouched nervously and gripped the sides, not at all sure she wanted to be part of Jug's Great Experiment.

Ellen's weight alone did no more to budge George than Jug's had. Jug added a brick, then another. The third one began to make a difference. The rope tightened and George and his platform appeared to lift a little. Encouraged, Jug plunked in two more and that did it. Ellen dropped and George was raised, his platform lurching and tipping.

Now George was as loyal a dog as any family could ever want, but aparently his loyalty oath hadn't covered any such emergency as this. "Hang on, George," commanded Jug, but George might not have heard him over Ellen's wails. As his unsteady perch tipped, the startled dog leaped for the ground and the platform shot up without him. Ellen descended just as fast and landed with a shattering crash and a scream for help that must have been heard clear to Arborley. The bucket came apart under the impact, George raced to the house away from the disaster, and Ellen sat on the ground in the wreckage. She was well cushioned with meadow grass and screaming her head off.

As it happened, Mr. Brown, the iceman, was just coming to the back door with a block of ice. George was too upset to watch where he was going. Mr. Brown went down, George went right through the mended screen door and Mama came running to see what had happened.

Mr. Brown wasn't hurt, he wasn't even mad. He jumped up, and abandoning the pile of ice on the doorstep, followed Mama up the hill to the orchard.

Papa heard the commotion and ran, too. He got there in time to hear Jug's explanation of the Great Experiment That Failed, and to make sure that Ellen wasn't hurt. She wasn't, only scared and furiously angry.

They tried not to laugh, but it struck them all so funny. Jug soon got over his disappointment and began to laugh, too, but not Ellen. She had had all the giggles knocked out of her.

It was a long while before she trusted her dolls to the mended bucket, and she insisted that she and she alone would handle the rope that hauled them up.

"For a little kid, you have some terrible ideas!" she said sternly. "If you're not careful, with ideas like that you'll end up in jail!"

George thought so, too, for all the coaxing in the world wouldn't make him visit the tree house again. Whenever they headed for the old orchard, George attended to his Mighty Hunter business in the other direction.

Chapter 9

Guy Hanley was a problem. The young Roosters knew it right away, and by the end of the week their parents knew it too. He was the fly in the ointment, the ant at the picnic, the one mosquito that managed to get in and spoil a night's sleep; he was the fifth wheel; he was everything that was unneeded and unwanted.

The only person who was wholeheartedly in favor of Guy Hanley was George. George poured out all the love in his doggy heart. Not that he neglected the others, he just added Guy to the list of people he adored. With George, Guy was likable and kind and patient and relaxed, all the things he wasn't with anyone else. It was a shame. With George he was almost human. But not with anyone else.

He was supercritical and let them know that Ramshackle Roost was far from the most deluxe place he had ever visited. He felt their family jokes were childish, apparently, and could just barely smile at the riddles that Jug and Ellen loved to ask. He was scornful of Hildy's inability to swim and of Mama's old-fashioned breast stroke. The only thing he seemed to enjoy was Mama's cooking, but he acted surprised that anyone's mother knew how to make pies and cakes. "We always had servants to do that," he said in a way that made Mama feel like a hired hand. He just didn't fit in.

Papa felt terrible, it was plain. After all, he was responsible for having Guy there, and if it didn't work out, and it wasn't going to, he was the one who would have to break the news to Professor Hanley. Hildy felt sorry for Papa, and then felt just as sorry for Spence and herself and all the rest of the family.

She thought about it that morning. It was a beautiful day, warm and sunny, and really she would have enjoyed playing stone stores with Ellen and Jug. But Guy was down there, fussing around on the end of the dock and making remarks about baby games, so she took the path through the woods to her rock.

The sky was a deep blue and the few little clouds were just for decoration. The air was like silk and the sun-warmed rock on which she lay felt good through her middy. Just warm, not hot. The small breeze carried scents that were new to her, sharp pungent smells of weeds and grasses and a faint sweetness that might be coming from the drifts of white flowers that foamed around the rock. Bees bumbled noisily in the blossoms, and across the field at the edge of the flowery meadow was a hedgerow of taller bushes. Birds flew in and out squabbling and singing.

She tried to think of a word to describe the perfection of the day and no words of her own could do it justice. But a poem they had learned in fifth grade said it all exactly.

" 'And what is so rare as a day in June?' " That had puzzled her. Weren't there thirty days in every June? Papa explained it. Rare in the poem meant very extra special.

> *Then, if ever, come perfect days*
> *Then Heaven tries the earth if it be in tune,*
> *And over it softly her warm ear lays.*

Miss Olmstead, their fifth grade teacher, was a great believer in memorizing poems. "Jewels of inspiration," she called them. "Priceless treasures to bring forth and enjoy when your own words are inadequate to describe a precious moment." Miss Olmstead got pretty gushy sometimes, really carried away. But in this case she was right. The poem said exactly what Hildy had wanted to say about this wonderful, perfect day.

In class Hildy dreaded reciting the poems she had learned. When she was called on she ducked her head and rattled off the verses in a monotone, da dum da dum da dum. But alone, out here in the meadow, the words came rolling out round and clear and lovely and just as beautiful as she always heard them in her head.

" 'Whether we look or whether we listen — ' " she fumbled aloud for the next line —

" 'We hear earth murmur or see it glisten,' " answered a voice from behind her. Hildy started and sat up indignantly. "What's the matter with you?" she asked. "It's not polite to sneak up on people!"

"Well, go on, what comes next?" When she did not continue, Guy asked, "What's the matter with *you?* Don't you remember what comes next?" Hildy didn't, and that made her madder.

"This is my private rock. I found it and it's mine."

"Don't be so touchy. Nobody wants your old rock. I just heard somebody reciting poetry and I wanted to find out who it was. Do you always talk to yourself?"

"I never talk to myself." That wasn't much of an answer, since that is just what she had been doing. "I sometimes say things out loud when I'm doing very private thinking all by myself." She said it pointedly enough. He got the hint. His fair skin flushed a bright red and he started to walk on.

From the hedgerow came a burst of singing that stopped him — glorious trills and bubbles of song that went up, up to the very top of heaven. Hildy held her breath, not wanting the slightest movement to disturb the singer. When it was over she let out her breath in a long sigh of pleasure.

"Meadowlark," Guy said briefly. He started to rustle off through the high grass.

"Wait," she called. "Was *that* what it was, a meadowlark?"

He did not turn back to look at her. "Meadowlark, male," he rattled off in a bored voice. "Back feathers brown streaked with black, brown, gray. Breast yellow, black crescent on throat. Nests on ground. Three to seven white eggs spotted with brown."

"Come back here," she commanded frantically. He had the answers to her questions and he was going away. "How do you know? Can you see him? How can you tell?"

He stopped. He didn't turn to look at Hildy, but he didn't go away. "How do you know?" she insisted.

"I know from the song, and from that I can tell the rest."

"How?"

"How? I *should* know how. I've been going to camp every summer since I was three and a half."

The way he said it, he didn't sound as if he was boasting. He sounded sad. She couldn't see his face but his back looked sad.

"Is that what you learn in camp, birds?"

"Birds and trees and wild flowers, Nature Study every day. Some of the camps were horse camps and some were for tennis and one was for making up school work so I wouldn't get left back. But every darn one of them had Nature Study."

"That sounds heavenly."

Guy shrugged. "It's O.K. the first few times around. But after a while you get to know all there is about an oak tree. After a while you get so you wish you'd never seen an oak tree or a woodpecker."

"I'd never get tired of that."

"You would if you had been sent away every summer since you were old enough to keep your pants dry. A summer is a long time to a little kid. Sometimes I used to get scared they'd never come to get me — " His voice trembled slightly and he hardened his tone quickly. "Not that I would have cared a lot," he said bitterly. "When they did come to take me home it was fight, fight all the time, real polite and mean, and then I'd get homesick for camp." He shrugged again as if to shake off a bad memory, and said in his usual scornful tone of voice, "What's all this bird business? You a bird watcher or something?"

"How can I watch birds if I don't know what I'm watching? Tell me about them, if you're so smart. How did you know for sure that was a meadowlark singing?"

"Be quiet a minute and listen, and I'll tell you."

They sat quietly as a bird began to trill again. When the singer was silent, Guy whistled a few bars of his song, not sweet and true, but the same little tune.

"Hear that? That's a song sparrow — out of season, though. In the early summer he sings louder and longer. He's — "

"Sshh — there he goes again!"

"Stupid. Not everything that sings is going to be a song sparrow, you know. That's a bluebird. The call goes 'tru-al-ly, tru-al-ly.' "

They listened again and this time instead of a bird song they heard the sound of the dinner bell. Its brassy clang was softened by the distance and it made Hildy think of *Heidi*, of goats pastured high in Alpine meadows. She hadn't realized it was so late. She sighed. She was hungry, as she always was at lunchtime, yet reluctant to leave her sunny flower-edged rock. Guy had already risen to go.

"Wait," she said urgently. "Will you teach me more after lunch. Promise?"

"More? You don't know *anything* yet." He was as patronizing as ever, as stuck-up as ever. Then he added, "I guess I might as well. No one else wants me around."

Hildy didn't know what to say. It was true, but she felt she should deny it, if only out of politeness. Truth won, so she answered simply, "Well, I do, if you'll tell me about birds."

He snorted and walked away. Hildy followed him happily along the path through the woods, stumbling occasionally because she was looking up into the trees, hoping to catch a glimpse of another bird.

"You'll have to learn to walk right if you're going to be a bird watcher. You can't crash along like that, falling all over your big feet."

An hour ago his superior tone would have irritated her into an angry reply. Now she accepted his criticism meekly and did her best to keep her eyes on the path. As they reached the back door, Guy said, "You don't need to yap about this, you know. I'll tell you about birds but you keep your mouth shut."

She nodded. If those were his terms, it was fine with her. So she said nothing, but she felt happy inside.

Chapter 10

I<small>T HAD BEEN</small> a good morning for everyone, apparently. It would have been hard not to have a good morning on such a beautiful day. Papa came whistling down from his upstairs workroom and Mama hummed as she made the sandwiches. Jug was as full of loud song as the meadowlarks. Mama had to protest, "Please Jug, don't talk with your mouth full."

"It's not talking, it's singing," he said thickly, through the peanut butter sandwich. A moment later he forgot and was again bellowing, "My country, 'tis of thee," with patriotic fervor. He stopped and asked:

"Who is Richard Stands, anyway? I always forget to ask."

"Who is who?"

"Richard Stands."

They all stared at him blankly.

"Rich-ard Stands! You know, the man who comes right after we sing 'My country, 'tis of thee.' I pledge my legions to the flag and to the country for Richard Stands!"

It was too much. No one meant to hurt Jug's feelings but it was just too much to hold in. They all roared, even Ellen, who wasn't sure just what was so funny. Mama laughed until she cried, and Hildy choked on her milk and had to have her back thumped.

"Oh, Jug! Richard Stands! The country for Richard Stands!" She hiccupped.

Jug's happy little face clouded over. He loved jokes but this hadn't been intended as a joke. Guy, who was sitting next to Jug surprised everyone by saying gently, "Don't feel too bad, Jug. Lots of people get things mixed up. I was in third grade before I caught on to 'My country 'tis of thee.' It didn't make any sense at all. I thought it was something about a big cake because we always sang 'of *the* icing.' I used to worry about it but I couldn't ask because everybody else in the class knew what it was all about."

The noisy table quieted down to hear what Guy was saying, and it stayed quiet. Hildy was a little ashamed that it was Guy who had comforted Jug while all the rest of them were laughing at him. Mama said gratefully, "You're right, Guy. I'll bet all of us had something we couldn't make head nor tails of when we were young."

And Papa added, "You're not alone, Jug. When all the others were in first grade they were always coming home with questions like that. The words are: 'I pledge *allegiance* to the flag and to the country for *which* it *stands*.' A perfectly natural mistake."

Jug felt better then and was able to smile again. There was a nice, pleased, friendly feeling all around the table, but when Hildy dared to smile across at Guy he answered her with a frosty glance that didn't invite friendship.

"Well," said Papa, when lunch and the few dishes were over. "I'm going to take a short nap in the hammock and then get back to work. What about the rest of you?"

"Tree house!" said Jug and Ellen together. Ellen added, "And then we'll go swimming and play stone stores."

"That sounds good," said Papa. "If I weren't so old and lazy I'd make a tree house for myself. Just don't put as much as a toe in the water — not even for stone stores — for a full hour, remember. Wait until you hear the bell."

Hildy raced to be first at the big flat rock in the meadow and sat down to wait for Guy. After what seemed like a very long wait she began to fidget. He *had* promised, hadn't he? Or did he mean sometime, not necessarily right after lunch. She tried to remember exactly how their conversation had gone, and couldn't. She had wrung a reluctant promise out of him, she was sure of that. But they hadn't discussed where they'd do their bird watching. Maybe he was waiting for her at the house, getting more annoyed with her by the minute. He didn't have much patience, Guy didn't.

She decided to give him a few more minutes. She lay down on the warm sunny rock with her head on her arm and counted slowly to one hundred and then a few more for good measure.

The sun had moved from high overhead and was now way over to one side, so low the daisies were casting a dappled shade over Hildy's face when she finally stirred. She groaned because the rock was so hard and lumpy, and the arm that was supporting her head was all pins and needles. She was stiff and sore and more than a little grouchy. That rotten Guy had wasted her entire afternoon, and from the looks of the sun, she had missed almost all the swimming time. Well, not swimming, but splashing, anyway. She was uncomfortably hot and sweaty and the thought of the cool river only made her feel worse.

She could hear Mama in the kitchen as she neared the back door. If it was that late, so late that Mama had been in and out, supper would be ready soon. There was no time to change into her suit so she clumped on down the flights of steps to the dock.

Ellen and Jug were so absorbed in their game of stone stores that they didn't even look up. Stone stores was a game Jug had invented the second day of their stay at Ramshackle Roost. The small beach and the riverbed were rocky. There were stones of all sizes, from little pebbles to great flat rocks like giant steppingstones. Some of the big ones thrust their tops out of the water, while the river eddied and flowed over others, and these others were the stone stores. The wares were stones, too, river-tumbled smooth stones of odd shapes and rich colors, stones that looked plain and dull when dried in the sun but when wet were veined and swirled with deep reds and greens. Patterned with moss, some of them, flecked with glitters of quartz, no two alike.

Each day's game began with a search for new treasures. No matter how many they found yesterday, Ellen and

Jug discovered new beauties under larger rocks, half covered with sand or washed onto the shore. They rinsed their finds, discarded any that turned out to be no more than ordinary, and arranged the rest lovingly where the clear water could flow over them, keeping them always bright and shining.

Then the bargaining began. They were scrupulously fair about taking turns and remembered from day to day just where they had left off. They bartered and haggled and exchanged — three red stripers for one that had a vein of pure gold running through it. Four fairly common greenies for one rare green with black ridges. And an even trade — the pale gray with a magic hole worn right through the middle for a guaranteed petrified midget dinosaur's egg.

Stone stores did not belong exclusively to Jug and Ellen. The others were welcomed, even urged to play. But Hildy couldn't enter into the bargaining with the deadly earnestness that the younger children demanded. She enjoyed lolling on her stone, feeling the cool water curl around her, poking at water bugs with a stick. They had no patience with her unbusinesslike attitude.

Still, for Hildy it was very satisfactory. She could enjoy the water fearlessly, lie right down in it and let it flow over her, and ignore the serious swimming that went on in the deep water at the end of the dock.

She had been determined to learn to swim this summer, had even planned her day-to-day progress in advance. According to her schedule she should have been swimming by now, but she had yet to make her first real attempt. She had counted on Spence to help her but he had no time to bother with her.

Spence and Guy were in fierce competition — not in the friendly matter-of-fact way that Ellen and Jug were competing for the best stones, but in a quite different, very personal way. It was not in the least friendly. When Spence cut the water in a smooth way, Guy's dive had to be smoother. If Guy could do the breast stroke without splashing, Spence tried to outdo him. They swam underwater until Hildy was afraid they might never come up. They rose to the surface at the same time, gulping for air. There was no time for lazy sunning or happy paddling.

Hildy stood on the dock, kicking an overturned row-boat with her sneakered foot, when Guy and Spence surfaced at the same time. They hauled themselves out of the water and stood shivering a little as they dried themselves. The shadow of the high bank stretched almost across the river now, and it was cool down here in the shade.

"Where were you?" Spence asked carelessly, not waiting for an answer. He flicked at her legs with his towel as he trotted past, headed for the steps.

She had made up her mind that she wouldn't mention the broken promise to Guy, not if her life depended on it. She wouldn't give him the satisfaction of knowing she was disappointed. He'd love it. She wouldn't say a word — and even as she was vowing this, she heard herself say, "I waited and waited."

There, she had done it again! Would she never learn

when to keep her mouth shut? Now she had set herself up for a sneering smart-aleck remark. She had deliberately asked for it.

Guy didn't answer right away. He scrubbed at his ears and dried his neck. Finally he said in a voice that was neither smart-aleck nor sneering, "I — I'm sorry. Spence asked me — Spence wanted to caulk the rowboats and it's a two-man job — "

Hildy understood. Spence, probably only because it was a two-man job and he wasn't sure how to do it, had made a friendly overture. Guy had decided to stick with Spence, of course. She couldn't exactly blame him. She followed him slowly up the steps feeling more left out than ever.

George took care of her left-out feeling. He came lunging down the steps, wildly happy to see her. He stopped long enough to sit down and fling a paw at Guy to be shaken, and hurried on to meet Hildy. It was good to be welcomed so wholeheartedly, and after she had been given several paw shakes and many wet kisses, they climbed the rest of the steps together.

"Anyway, I've got you, George." His long pink tongue lolled out of his mouth as he smiled up at her. Whatever happened, there was always George.

Supper was great. Mama had already set the table out on the front porch with a big bunch of daisies in the center in one of Ramshackle Roost's many cut-glass bowls, and a tiny bouquet of daisies at each place. The whole house smelled heavenly. Something good had been baking but Mama wouldn't tell what.

"Just you wait and see." Well, it was worth waiting

for. When it was time for dessert Mama came out from the kitchen carrying the most enormous pie anyone had ever seen. Ramshackle Roost was used to crowds, and there was this enormous pie pan in the cupboard just begging to be used, and those blackberries practically falling off the bushes, Mama explained. She showed her many scratches from the blackberry stickers as proudly as if she had just won an award for bravery.

"The cut glass was a challenge," she explained. "It was so dull and greasy and dusty, and now, doesn't it look lovely?"

It really did. The big elaborate punch bowl glittered in the last light of the sun and each little daisy-filled salt shaker sparkled. The pie plates were cut glass, too, as fancy as they could be. It made it seem just like a party.

"I thought you were going to take it easy," Papa remarked. "I understood we were going in for simplified living this summer. This is *simplified?*"

"Couldn't help it," Mama explained. "Every time I looked at that great ugly monster of a cookstove laughing at me, I knew I'd have to master it or die trying. I kicked it and beat it with the poker until finally the oven heated up to what felt like pie-baking temperature, and now we both know who's boss in that kitchen."

"I forbid you," said Papa, "I absolutely forbid you to work so hard on your vacation. But since you regard this as some sort of a crazy challenge, not work — do you suppose I could have another piece of pie?"

There was enough pie for seconds all around, and they sat there breathing heavily and loosening belts while the light faded out of the sky and they could no longer see the silvery flash of the river down below.

They could hear it, though, a soft rippling soothing sound that flowed on and on. The twilight was full of the small scratchings and twitterings of birds as they settled down for the night. From somewhere came the liquid song of a bird that wasn't ready for sleep.

"Mockingbird," said Guy quietly to Hildy. He hadn't changed his mind about bird watching, then. He remembered!

As it grew darker there was a glittering of lightning bugs all around the porch, more and more of them, whole swarms flicking their little switches on and off. Lightning bugs were no strangers to Cutler Street, but they never came in such numbers as this. The younger children were off in a flurry of old jelly glasses, but Hildy had no desire to join them. Let the little ones run and chase and capture the magic if they could — she was content to watch.

"It's cold light," Spence explained. "Nobody's quite sure how they do it."

Hildy didn't care. She had no need of facts or explanations. It was enough that lightning bugs — no, fireflies was a prettier name — that fireflies were here, poking holes in the purple dusk, scattering little sprinkles of enchantment.

"They light as they fly up," she discovered. "All the little lights are moving upward. Fireflies light on the rise," she repeated to herself. "Fireflies light on the rise."

It seemed like a momentous discovery, like an omen of happier things coming.

Chapter 11

"Lookit the moon!" Jug pointed, and they all watched as the moon seemed to break loose from the dark trees across the river and float up to a clear place in the sky. It looked pale and misty and an orange halo encircled it.

"Looks funny to me," Jug said, "like it's sick maybe."

Papa leaned back in his porch rocker.

"It means rain is coming," he said. "Ring around the moon, wet weather soon."

Spence didn't agree. "That's not scientific, Papa. That's just something people say."

"A lot you know," Guy answered him quickly. "It's been established that a lot of those old sayings are true — red sky at night, sailor's delight — and things like that. It's going to rain!"

"Oh boy, old Mr. United States Weather Bureau himself!" Spence felt like bickering.

Papa said gently, "Why don't we wait and see? If it rains in a day or so, we'll know the ring around the moon was right."

It seemed as if it would never rain again. One beautiful flawless day had followed another. The sun shone, the birds sang, the Ramshackle Roosters went their various ways and all were happy. Even Guy was no longer considered a menace. Sometimes he was only tolerated, but most of the time he was almost liked. As each weekend came and went and Professor Hanley came to visit, no one insisted that he take his grandson home. Spence needed his help with the boats and Hildy was not about to give up her bird lessons.

Sometimes Guy was pretty hard to take, and then trouble would break out again. Like the time Spence and Guy had to make repeated trips into Arborley for supplies for the boat work. If they got an early enough start they could meet Mr. Brown at the end of the lane as he went by to the ice house in Arborley to get his day's supply. They would do their shopping while the wagon was being loaded, and be ready to ride out again.

Spence always enjoyed the leisurely trip, the many stops along the way and Mr. Brown's funny stories, which were as long and rambling as his delivery route. But it made Guy edgy. He always had to make it clear to the people in the hardware store, and even to Mr. Brown, that he usually traveled in a touring car, not in an ice wagon. Then Spence would cut him down to size, and Guy would sulk, and the unpleasantness would hang in the air like a dark cloud, spoiling everyone's fun.

It was like that the day they first saw the poster in a store window announcing the Firemen's Carnival in August. There was to be a merry-go-round, and booths and games and prizes. It sounded like fun.

Guy, of course, had assumed that they would all go.

Mama said, "No, Guy, I don't think we will. We — well, we just can't afford it, that's all. We agreed when we rented the Roost that we wouldn't spend any extra money for recreation. We've already spent more than we planned getting the place fixed up and the boats ready. But never mind, we can do things at home that will be cheap and fun."

"For Pete's sake," said Guy, "it's only fifty cents to get in and ten cents for each ride or game — "

"No, Guy." Mama was firm, with that tone in her voice that meant: Don't argue with me. Hildy knew it well, but Guy went right on.

"Aw gee, *anybody* has fifty cents, for heaven's sake! Let me pay everybody's way, then, and you won't have to worry about it."

"I'm not in the least worried. I'm not even going to give it a second thought," Mama said pleasantly. Guy had really fixed things, the bigmouth! His chances of getting to the carnival were never good, but now they were nil. Oh, well. Hildy put the Firemen's Carnival out of her mind and picked up her bag of groceries.

Guy hadn't forgotten it, though. From time to time he hinted that he had plans to go anyway, they'd see. He evidently wasn't accustomed to being told that he couldn't do something, and the idea that people might not be able

to afford extra treats was entirely new to him. Hildy and
Spence wanted to go, too, and it didn't help to have their
visitor harping on the subject.

The bird lessons went on, not often enough to satisfy
her, but often enough that she could now make a list of
familiar birds and listen with delight to their calls. Guy
gave the information sort of grudgingly and warned her
crossly, "There's not much singing going on in the summer, you know, so don't expect to hear all these birds any
time you want." But at the same time that he complained,
he told her about flowers and trees and mushrooms and
bugs, and that was good, too. He acted glad that she asked.
He was a funny mixture of nasty and nice.

She thought about this while Spence and Guy were
arguing about the rain. She didn't want it to rain, for

goodness' sake, and yet she hoped that Guy was right about the weather. If he was right about birds and mushrooms, he should know about weather, too. But weather was scientific, she knew, they talked about it in school. Barometers and atmosphere and things, so maybe Spence knew best because he liked scientific things. It was hard to decide which one she wanted to be right.

As it turned out, the moon backed Guy and Papa's theory — or was it the other way around? Anyway, the next morning the wet weather arrived.

Hildy woke very early, and for a moment she didn't know where she was. Everything was wrapped in a moist woolly mist. She could see the hump that was Ellen beside her, and the porch railing, and beyond that — nothing. The trees had disappeared in the fog. After weeks of warm sunshine, she was chilled. She was glad to slide down under her blanket. But even the blanket was clammy, and after a few minutes she decided to get dressed and explore a little.

She moved quietly — no need to wake the others if they could sleep a little longer. Besides, it was a nice feeling to be the only one in the whole Roost who was awake. It was like being alone on a desert island.

Floorboards creaked under her careful feet, and out on the north porch George thumped his tail and moaned in his sleep. She waited a moment but he sighed and snored on, so she tiptoed through the dark kitchen and out the back door. The screen door flapped noisily behind her, as loud as could be in the mysterious quiet, but no one stirred.

Everything was wet, pearled with drops of mist. Almost

without thinking she took the path that led to her flowery meadow, and then wondered at her own bravery. When she first came to Ramshackle Roost, the woods seemed dark and forbidding, like the deep forest in a Grimm's fairy tale. At first she had been timid, fearful of going too far alone. And now look at scaredy Hildy Stuart, she marveled, going off alone in the fog and nobody even knows she's gone. She had come a long way, she thought, exceedingly pleased with herself.

The fog muffled sounds. Her footsteps on the damp leaves made no noise at all, and a squirrel's chatter overhead sounded faint and far away. The world had shrunk to a very small circle and Hildy was at the silent center of it.

When the trees opened out into the meadow, the foggy world grew no larger. Close at hand, daisy heads were dripping with heavy dew. The bright blue flowers that Guy had told her were chicory were closed tight. No sun. That's what Guy said they did on sunless days.

She was moving toward her special flat rock when a sound behind her stopped her in her tracks. Someone was coming — someone was quite near! She had thought she was so brave, but the quiet approach of the Something turned her to ice. The high rock where Ellen played must be nearby — but where? She had lost her bearings turning around so suddenly like that. If she stood very still — didn't even breathe —

With a happy *Rumpf!* the Something burst out of the fog and Hildy started to breathe again.

"Oh, you fool!" she said, more to herself than to George as she shook his large damp paw. "You big stupid booby!"

Delighted that he had tracked her successfully, George licked her face and left paw prints all over her clean middy.

"You awful smelly horrible creature," she giggled. "You almost scared me out of my wits."

Now that she wasn't scared anymore, she realized that she was hungry. Ravenous, starving. "Hurry," she said to George, "we'll be late for breakfast. Gooey will eat your bone!"

They burst into the kitchen together, and the screen door slammed behind them. Mama jumped at the sound. She was down on her knees, fighting with the stove which wouldn't light properly. She looked up and said, through clenched teeth, "I'm giving this monster one more chance and then I'll beat it to junk with the poker! Why I ever thought this would be a vacation — I must have been out of my mind!"

Guy was trying to help, making sympathetic noises which Hildy knew would only infuriate Mama further.

Mama said to the stove, "One of us has got to go, and we'll settle this right now!"

Guy looked sort of scared and worried, but the Stuart children weren't at all concerned. Mama always acted this way when any sort of appliance wouldn't work. She took it as a personal insult.

"We've got plenty of corn flakes," said Hildy. "We don't need the stove."

Papa had come downstairs whistling. He stood watching and grinning with his hands in his pockets.

"You know Mama doesn't feel up to joining the human race until she's had her first cup of coffee — "

111

Mama answered coldly, "Don't you dare make a joke of this, Paul Stuart. It is a very serious matter. Our entire welfare depends on getting this — *thing* — to burn. It is wet and miserable outside."

"A great example of logic, my dear," said Papa. "What has the weather outside to do with your battle in here with the stove?"

"It's perfectly clear to me!" yelled Mama, and she gave the stove a mighty belt with the poker. Something inside jiggled and fell into place, and a small flame licked around the piece of kindling. They all watched hopefully while Mama added a few more pieces of wood and were pleased to see the small flame burst into a large blaze. Mama smiled triumphantly, replaced the stove lid, and set the coffeepot on with a bang.

"There," she said, every inch a winner. "We've settled that. I'll have my coffee. Now for the oatmeal and cocoa."

No one protested the change in the menu. The hot cereal would be very welcome. It wasn't so cold outside, but inside the Roost it felt cold and clammy, and the dampness brought out the smell of skunk from under the kitchen floor. Mama was right — the heat of the stove did help and it was worth the struggle.

The Stuarts took Mama's outburst of temper in their stride, and once it was over, didn't give it a second thought. They were used to it. The nice thing about Mama was that she could get good and mad about *things,* but she was easygoing about people.

But Guy was subdued. He really looked absolutely shaken. Evidently no one in his family ever kicked a balky washing machine nor whacked the carpet sweeper.

Hildy wondered how his mother dealt with a washing machine whose motor would not start. Some other way, apparently. Probably called the butler, she decided. Anyway the stove fixing had left him upset, as if Mama was going to be mad at him, too. When she announced cheerfully after breakfast that there would be an expedition into Arborley for groceries, and all helping hands would be welcome, he declined to go.

"I'll stay here and work on the boats," he said nervously.

"Can't do anything until we get some more sandpaper and the right kind of paint, but I can pick that out," said Spence.

"You'll both go," Mama decided. "We'll have a lot of bags to carry."

"I hope Mr. Brown isn't a racing driver," said Papa. "The fog is too thick for speeding." Papa was always happy in the morning these days. His book was going well and he could hardly wait to get upstairs to his workroom to begin on the next chapter. Sometimes when ideas were coming thick and fast he made a sandwich in the morning and ate it at his typewriter instead of coming down for lunch. When he was stuck, they would hear him pacing the floor, round and round the little room, until he worked out the part that was bothering him.

Ellen wanted to go along and help with the shopping but Jug was not interested.

"I have to try out my tree house in the fog," he explained. "I never had a foggy tree house in my whole life."

"Then you must stick around and keep an eye on him, Hildy." He set up a howl and Mama gave in. "All right,

you don't have to keep an eye right *on* him, just be here
to call for Papa if he should break his leg or get bitten by
a rattlesnake. Once he gets going, Papa doesn't hear anything. The house could fall down and he'd never know
it."

For once Hildy didn't mind in the least being left behind. She was glad to see the shoppers disappear around
the bend in the lane. Jug hurried off to the tree house in
the orchard, George went the other way to hunt rabbits,
and Papa's typewriter began clacking away up in his workroom. That left Hildy in charge of everything.

With all the beautiful weather they had enjoyed, every
inch of the riverbank, the woods, the orchard had been
explored. But Ramshackle Roost, except for the rooms
that were used every day, was almost unknown territory,

and Hildy decided it was high time she explored that too.

The kitchen skunk smell didn't penetrate to the third floor, but there was another smell that they didn't notice when all the windows were open and a breeze was blowing in. It was a dead musty smell of things long unused. A haunted house smell, Hildy decided. Her footsteps echoed along the empty hall. It would have been downright spooky if it hadn't been for the distant tap of the typewriter.

The hall in the front of the third floor was wide and fairly light, for it opened on an upstairs porch. But when the hall turned and became narrow and dark, she felt as if she were miles away from everything.

She opened a door, not boldly at all, but timidly. She knew, of course, that she would find nothing there, nothing but a jumble of old-fashioned furniture. Nothing interesting. But as she closed the door again, something somewhere made a noise. The old house groaned, a floorboard squeaked, some perfectly reasonable sound, she told herself sternly. She tried not to notice the shiver that ran up her back.

She recalled something out of a long-forgotten book, all about a man in a long cloak who followed people about in the halls of a castle. They felt his presence but when they turned, no matter how quickly, he had darted out of sight. She wasn't sure she had read it — maybe she was making it up; or maybe there was someone — she whirled around, and wouldn't have been surprised to see the edge of a black cloak disappearing into a doorway.

Of course the hallway was empty. She stood still for a

long time listening to the pounding of her heart, and finally was calm again.

"Look here," she said to herself, "either you go on exploring, or go back downstairs and sit in the kitchen and shake until they all come home. Are you a man or a mouse?"

She giggled and said aloud, "Mouse!" The sound of her voice was reassuring. She felt brave enough to open the next door. These bedrooms must have been the less expensive ones for the summer boarders. They were small and furnished with odds and ends of uncomfortable furniture. Still, people probably spent most of their time outside or on the porches, and a cramped little room didn't matter.

"Seen one, you've seen 'em all," she said. Two rooms were enough and she was glad to hustle down the stairs to the second floor. Still, she had stuck it out even when she was scared. She hadn't run away. It was another small victory for Scaredy-Cat Hildy, and she felt good about it.

Next to Papa's workroom was a small corner room. Hildy remembered it from the first day when she had carried all those loads of old magazines up from the living room. She opened the door quietly, so as not to disturb Papa's train of thought. There they were, all those old magazines, going back forever and ever to the old days.

She blew the dust off the first magazine, sneezed, wiped her nose on the tail of her middy blouse and settled down. After the first few pages she wanted to bang on the wall and shout for Papa. The pictures were so funny — did people ever really wear clothes like that? She giggled, but quietly, for Papa had hit a snag again. The typing stopped and she could hear his footsteps, up and down, round and round the room. This was no time to interrupt his work. She could share the pictures later.

Before she knew it, it was already later. The back door slammed, there were shouts and sounds of cupboard doors banging. Jug's and of course George's ears were keenly attuned to the arrival of food. In a moment she heard Jug boom, "When do we eat?"

It was a good question, Hildy decided, and one her stomach had been asking for some while. High time it got an answer.

Chapter 12

THE FOG turned into rain, rain that went on and on and on. The first day indoors had a kind of novelty, and it wasn't too hard to keep everyone occupied and happy. Mama went on a cooking binge, and that was fine. Spence and Guy were glad to bring wood from the woodshed if it meant batches of cookies. But after a while even cookies, good as they were, were not enough.

The large dining room rang with shouts and screams and giggles. Rope-jumping, and hopscotch chalked right on the floor. They played hide-and-seek all over the house until Papa made the second floor out of bounds because he couldn't hear himself think.

By the fifth day the games were over. Everyone was thoroughly fed up with everyone else. The smell of old skunk got worse instead of better, sheets were clammy and uncomfortable, the upstairs bedrooms seemed like prisons after the freedom of sleeping out on the porch. Mama had to fight every day to start the stove and that made for a lot of confusion. Even Ellen's dolls were mad at one another.

With Spence and Guy it was even worse. They could hardly look at each other without making some kind of insulting remark. The rivalry that usually simmered below the surface came to a full rolling boil. Their unpleasantness spoiled things for everyone else, and by the end of the fifth rainy day the Ramshackle Roosters were just barely speaking.

Except for Papa, whose book ideas were coming fast and who hardly knew night from day when he was writing, and for George, whose good-natured kisses were always the same — except for these two the Ramshackle Roosters were an unhappy, unfriendly group.

"Well, now," said Papa cheerily on the fifth evening, "let's not just mope around. How about we sit by the fire and sing?"

"We've run out of logs," mumbled Spence. "We have to keep all the dry wood for the kitchen stove."

"We haven't run out of voices, have we? Come on, let's have a rousing chorus of — "

No one wanted to join him in a rousing chorus of anything.

"Checkers?" he asked hopefully after a while.

"George ate three red checkers and a black one," said Hildy, "and serves him right if he throws up."

"Which he will probably choose to do on my bed," said Mama. George snuggled closer to her and she wrinkled her nose at the pungent doggy odor. There was another period of silence, and then Mama, who thought food was a natural cure for all ailments, large or small, got her bright idea.

"I have it!"

"Some rare jungle disease, probably, and we'll all catch it," said Spence. "What is it?"

"I won't tell until it's ready. Just come when I call."

They sat around in clouds of gloom while Mama made interesting sounds out in the kitchen. There was the noise of kindling being slammed into the stove and a cheerful banging of stove lids. Soon a sweet warm gingery smell came into the living room, but pleasant as it was, no one brightened noticeably. Finally she rang the dinner bell. In answer to its insistent clang they filed reluctantly into the kitchen. No one was going to cheer up the Roosters if they could help it.

"It's cooked," reported Mama happily. "And I've put it out to cool, and in a few minutes we can pull it."

"*Pull* it? Pull what?"

"Taffy. Delicious molasses taffy. It says here" — she consulted her cookbook — " 'With greased hands pull the taffy until it is smooth and straw-colored.' "

"Yechch!"

"Yechch me no yechch's. Just grease your hands and do as I say. Come on, butter them!"

Groaning, they rubbed a little butter on their hands while Mama scooped up lumps of taffy from the platters where it was cooling. Ellen and Hildy were first. Hildy yelled that it was too hot and Ellen added that it was too sticky, but once they were into it they had no choice except to follow Mama's commands.

120

"Now, pull," she said. "Keep kneading it together and then pull it out into a rope. It says here it gets lighter in color and smoother the longer you work it."

It did smell good and it was something to do, at least. Much better than just sitting around griping. Papa pulled with Jug. Spence and Guy hadn't intended to cooperate at all, but Mama plopped a gob of taffy in Spence's hand and pushed Guy into it. They glared at each other as they struggled with the sticky mess.

"You didn't butter your hands enough," said Mama. "Here."

Papa began to sing a sea chanty and to pull with real vigor, and Jug had to pull back to keep up with him. Soon they were all giggling and singing — except Spence and Guy. But the taffy won out over both of them. First it stuck and they had to scrape each other loose. Then when

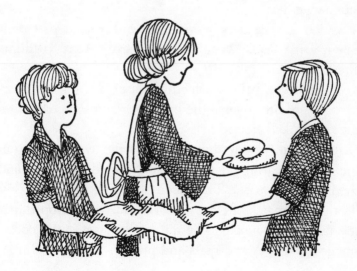

they were cleaned off and buttered thoroughly and pulling away, mad as two wet hens, the molasses taffy began to turn smooth. Each pull made it lighter in color and easier to work. They pulled so hard that their glob turned into candy long before any of the others could see results. At last, exhausted, they put their rope of taffy on the greased platter again and Mama cut it into bite-sized pieces. Each boy wore a sheepish grin. Some kind of armistice had been declared.

They were all so busy pulling that no one noticed George until he began to whine in a strangled muffled sort of way. Since no one offered him any, George had helped himself to a generous portion of taffy, and now he was sorry. Guy held George while Spence pried open his jaws and scraped the gummy mess off his teeth, and George did his best to get away. In a situation like that, it was impossible not to be friendly, and when George was finally cleaned up and could bark again, both boys could laugh together.

When all the taffy was pulled and a good part of it eaten, Papa said, "Would you believe it? It's bedtime already."

"Would you believe something else? I think it's clearing up." Mama opened the back door and stepped out on the rain-soaked ground.

It was still cloudy, but gusts of wind were pulling at the clouds, tearing off wisps that obscured the moon and then blew on past. The moon was pale and wan, but floating in a patch of clear sky. The trees still dripped, but the rain had stopped. The air smelled wet and woodsy, smelled of leaves and grass and puddles and good things.

They could hear the rush of the rain-swollen river, and somewhere a grateful bird chirped.

"We can sleep out again!" shouted Jug. "Let's make up our beds!"

There was a dash for the stairs. Guy and Spence hung back. The matter of sleeping on the porch had never been mentioned — Spence was too stubborn to extend the invitation and Guy too proud to say he'd like to sleep down there, too. After all this long time it was not easy to bring it up. Spence shuffled his feet in embarrassment and then said quickly, "Get your blankets, Gooey. It's too stuffy to sleep inside."

They were off in a flash.

"Well!" said Papa. "Looks like you started more than a taffy pull tonight, Sara. Peace has been declared."

"Enjoy it, but don't count on it. The truce may not last until morning."

But the truce did last. It lasted through the last days of July and into August. If there were fights and disagreements — and there were, of course — they were soon forgotten in the rush of all the things that still remained to be done. Before the spell of rainy weather, the summer stretched out endlessly before them all. They had forever ahead of them. When the sun shone again, things had changed. The air seemed thicker and sweeter, the trees were heavy with summer. Few birds sang under the broiling sun, nesting time was past. The young birds had learned their lessons and were flying about on their own.

The meadow bloomed furiously, almost frantically, and on the evening air was a new fragrance of hayfield and sweet clover. There was an urgency in the singing of the katydids. The Ramshackle Roosters began to count the days, regretfully, that were left to them. No day was ever long enough, and it seemed a shame to waste a minute in eating or sleeping. Yet how good the eating was, and how deep their sleep.

The sun soon dried out the rowboats and Spence and Guy painted as fast as they could. Because the time was running out they even let Hildy paint, and she labored gladly in the heat. They planned as they painted — races, picnics on the opposite shore, a trip upriver to explore the shallow rapids a mile or two above their house. There was a little island, too. Mr. Brown, the iceman, told them about it. It had a small sandy beach where vacationers years ago used to gather for beach parties. It was all there waiting for them but they had to hurry, hurry, before it was too late.

Jug and Ellen were elected to entertain George while all the painting was going on. Since it never occurred to George that he was not a person, he wanted to help with every interesting detail. It was easy to imagine what he would do with opened cans of paint. Jug and Ellen did their job well, and they managed to finish with only a streak of blue on George's back.

They decided that the boats should be named the *Niña*, *Pinta* and *Santa Maria*, and Hildy was chosen to paint the names in shaky lettering. It was pretty bad, but no one was about to quibble over perfection now when time was growing so short.

Spence had taken the lead in caulking and painting the boats. He was quick to do things with his hands and used tools much more expertly than Guy. But when all the repairs were made and two of the boats were ready for launching, Guy took over. After all, he had rowed boats at summer camps for years, and Spence had never even been out in a boat. Pitman Pond had given him no nautical experience at all.

It took a whole morning of humiliation, of frustration and floundering before he could row in a straight line, with only a glance over his shoulder to make sure he was aiming right. He pulled too hard or not hard enough, dipped too deep or not deep enough, and Guy corrected him patiently.

In a way, the last few days had been the happiest of all for Hildy. Her help was needed and so for once she was part of the group. While Spence was learning to row, Hildy sat facing him in the back of the boat, which Guy insisted they must call the stern, and helped with the steering.

"A little more to the right, no left — left — my right, your left — oh, drat it, now pull the other way."

Guy rowed easily alongside and shouted directions. Hildy itched to try. She knew, she was *positive* she knew how to do it if only she could get her hands on the oars. But it was Spence's turn first. By afternoon the freshly painted third boat should be dry enough to put in the water and Hildy would get her turn.

By noon Spence had two handfuls of blisters and aching shoulders, but at lunch he was able to announce, "I did it! I can row!"

Everybody cheered. There were immediate plans for a picnic that very afternoon, and an expedition to the island upstream. And then Papa made the remark that ruined everything for Hildy.

"No nonswimmers out in the boat."

When Papa made his announcement, Hildy, Spence and Guy all yelled together, "What?" but Hildy was screeching the loudest.

"I said" — Papa raised his voice to be heard over the noise — "no nonswimmers may go out in the boats. That was one of the first water rules we decided on," he continued reasonably, "and one of the smartest." He went on with his eating as if nothing had happened, just as if the world had not suddenly come to an end.

"But, but," sputtered Hildy, "I've been out in a boat the whole morning! Nothing happened — see — I didn't drown!"

"Don't force your luck," said Papa. "Next time you might. You were breaking the rules, you realize, but we'll let it go this time. Just don't do it again."

"I can go," bellowed Jug happily. "I can swim!" And so he could. It wasn't good swimming, and like everything else he did, it was noisy, but he could keep himself afloat. So could all the others, Hildy realized miserably. Mama swam a dignified slow old-lady kind of breast stroke, and Ellen was still doggy-paddling, but if she had to she could splash to shore.

"I won't stand up in the boat," she promised fervently. "Never! I'll sit square in the middle. I won't fool around — "

"You won't get the chance. May I have another sandwich, Sara? I have an enormous appetite today."

Hildy had lost her appetite. She had a great big lump

in her throat that wouldn't go down and she blinked hard to keep from crying.

"Sorry, Hildy. I know it's a disappointment, but that's the way the world goes, sometimes." She could hardly believe it. Papa was acting like a — a horrible, hateful — she couldn't think of a word mean enough to describe his behavior.

Chapter 13

DO MY EYES deceive me? Am I really receiving some very dirty looks?"

Hildy almost choked. Here the worst thing in the world had happened to her and Papa was acting as if it was some kind of private joke.

"P-papa!" she sputtered.

"Don't be so indignant, Hildy. You've known from the day we arrived that nonswimmers were not to go out in the boats. But you chose to be a nonswimmer, so it's your own doing. And let me remind the rest of you" — here he looked sternly over his glasses at the others — "another rule we agreed upon is that if one person disobeys the water rules and any of the others knows about it and remains silent — all of you, *every single one of you* will stay out of the water for the rest of the summer. Is that clear? And now, if I may be excused, I have some work to do."

He left the rest of the Ramshackle Roosters sunk in gloom.

"Aw heck, Hildy, I'll bet you'd really like to see that desert island up the river," said Jug.

"Don't worry, Hildy, I'll tell you all about it, every single thing," Ellen comforted her.

Even Guy was sympathetic. "That's too bad, Hildy. It was your turn to learn to row next. It's really too bad."

Too bad? It was the end of the world, that's all it was!

Suddenly Spence spoke up. "We'd better get moving. We've got only a couple of hours if Hildy's going to be swimming by tomorrow morning."

An astonished silence followed this remark. Then Mama said, "But she's afraid of the water, Spence."

"O.K., she'll be a scared swimmer. Papa didn't say she had to like it. Gooey, you've been to all those camps and had lots of lessons — how do we begin?"

"Spence, you're crazy! She can't learn to swim in one afternoon! It takes weeks!"

"We haven't got weeks. All we have is this one afternoon. After that, if she can't swim she'll have to stay home. Come on, what's the best way to begin? How do those swimming instructors at all those camps begin? Get into your suit, Hildy, and let's go."

"Now you wait a minute, young man," said Mama. "Nobody goes into the water for an hour yet. And don't you go scaring Hildy to death, either. Never mind, lovey, we'll find something nice to do while the others are out in the boats. Maybe we could go into Arborley for ice-cream cones."

"Mama!" Spence's voice rose and cracked, he was so

exasperated. "Mama, just once will you believe that food won't fix everything? I don't care how many ice-cream cones she eats, Hildy's got to get up off her duff and *swim!*"

They all looked at Hildy. After a moment she said in a quavery voice, "I'll — I'll get my suit on. It's all right, Mama, honest."

"You can't go in for an hour," Mama yelled over the noise they were all making. Spence gave in on that one point, but on everything else he overrode every objection and swept them all down to the dock to get ready for the swimming lesson as soon as the hour was up.

Guy was protesting, too. He insisted that all good teachers got their students used to the water gradually, let them play and splash and get confidence first.

"Hildy's been playing and splashing for years. If she hasn't got any confidence now she'll have to swim without it. This is her last chance. Go on in, Hildy, the hour's up."

She waded in, cautiously and fearfully as always, hating that awful moment when the water first rose around her stomach. But Spence would not give her time to dread it. "Duck! No, do it again, all the way down! Every bit of your head under!"

Spence bullied and shouted, and the others coaxed and comforted and advised, and Hildy tried to obey all the orders and suggestions, no matter who said what. She floundered and spluttered and gulped water and spit it out, and somehow in the confusion she found herself floating, first face down and then face up, then with her legs thrashing and her arms extended. Then her arms

130

would work right but she'd forget to kick or to breathe.

From time to time, Mama hauled her out and dried her face and insisted that she be given a moment to rest. Spence allowed her only a moment and then he hurried her in again.

She cut her knee on a sharp rock, but it soon stopped bleeding in the cold water. It would have made no difference if it hadn't stopped, for by now even Hildy had caught Spence's determination. She was too rushed and harried to think about being afraid, and as Spence gradually moved her out into deeper water she was only glad that she didn't seem to kick her feet against the rocks so often.

She was so tired and so waterlogged and so confused that when all at once everyone began yelling the same thing instead of five different orders at once, she really didn't catch what they were screaming.

"Hildy's swimming! Hildy's swimming!" She could hear Jug's bellow above all the rest and all of a sudden she realized what he was saying. She was swimming! She had gone five whole strokes with her feet off the bottom and no helping hands clutching her middle. She was swimming! In her excitement she gulped in when she should have blown out, and the hands were there again, holding her up and pulling her over to the dock. She was in deep water, and she was swimming — or had been — for several minutes.

"You did it! You did it!" Mama, when she was excited, could make as much noise as Jug. Hildy climbed the ladder and flopped down on the dock, gasping. Someone rubbed her dry with a towel, and when she stopped panting she sat up and grinned. She had swallowed so much water she gurgled when she moved, but it didn't matter. Nothing mattered. Hildy could swim.

After she had rested she was ready to try again. Mama sent Ellen up to get Papa. "Just this once we'll interrupt his work," she said. "This is important."

Papa came down the steps, as excited as everyone else. His face was shining with pride as she swam her shaky five strokes again. Only this time she stretched it to six and then to seven. She was trying for ten but her arms and legs refused to cooperate. Hildy was all in, and no wonder.

"Let's all get out and let Hildy rest," suggested Mama.

"No, no, I'm afraid I'll forget — "

"You'll never forget now," Papa assured her. "How

about this for a plan? A good rest for everybody and sup-per very early, and we'll still have time for another lesson before dark."

It sounded like a good plan, and it was. Hildy slept like a log in the hammock. The warm sunshine dried out her water-soaked body and she felt like a new person when the dinner bell rang. She was a new person. The new Hildy Stuart who had learned to swim. Nothing would ever be as hard again.

Chapter 14

THEN THE SUMMER really began to slide away from them in a mad rush. There was so much to do and time was running out. Papa agreed that Hildy's swimming, while not good, was good enough to get by, provided she practiced every chance she got. So every morning before breakfast she and Spence and Guy plunged into the cold river and practiced faithfully. The hour after breakfast was spent in a slapdash rush of bed-making, dish-washing, wood-chopping, and then down to the river again for rowing lessons. They all learned, even Ellen and Jug. And when the hour was up and Mama brought the lunch basket, they set off to explore in the *Niña*, the *Pinta* and the *Santa Maria*.

"Don't forget that hour after lunch," Mama warned. "Be careful, use your common sense, and be home by suppertime."

Spence and Ellen and the lunch rode in the flagship. Guy was captain of the *Pinta* with Jug as crew, and Hildy was responsible for the little blue *Niña* with George as lookout.

George, they discovered, was an explorer at heart. He took to the water as if he had been a seafarer all his life. He barked when it seemed necessary but he neither romped nor lurched in the boat. He sat solemn and dignified and thumped his tail occasionally to show his pleasure. Once, when the *Pinta* pulled close alongside, he did lean far over to shake hands with Jug, but as the rowboat rocked he quickly shifted his weight until it was steady again.

"He's a salty old sea dog," shouted Jug. "Admiral George!"

They went upstream to the little island Mr. Brown had told them about. It was hard to row against the current, but by staying close to the bank where the river rippled gently instead of rushing, they were able to manage.

The island was tiny, with a miniature beach and a small grove of trees for shade. It was beautiful and quiet and exactly the right size. Not so small as to be crowded, nor so big that Jug and Ellen could get lost. At its farthest edge Hildy was only a shout and a short walk from the others. George covered it in a few happy leaps.

They swam — paddled and waded mostly, for the water curled at the edge of the island in little shallow rills — and ate and swam again after a suitable time had passed. They watched the sun drop lower behind the trees and knew that they soon must leave. Jug insisted on one last dip and when they had dried off a little, they knew they *really* must leave, much as they all hated to go.

"Good-bye, desert island," Ellen called. "We'll be back."

Hildy felt a shiver of lovely sadness, a shiver that had nothing to do with the damp hair dribbling down her back. They would come back, of course, but never again would it be for the first time on a voyage of discovery.

When the *Niña*, the *Pinta* and the *Santa Maria* were pushed away from the shallows and into the current, the hurrying river kept them all busy. Hildy had no time to enjoy her sadness, or even to give the island one last look for good luck. The river rushed them along so fast there was not much need for rowing. Spence and Hildy and Guy had to be alert to pull on an oar to steer off the rocks and shoals. Jug and Ellen were lookouts. Hildy followed in the wake of the other two boats, nervously zigging and zagging and expecting any minute to hear the crunch of wood on rock. She heaved a deep sigh of relief when they pulled out of the current and over to the quiet water of Ramshackle Roost's dock. Papa and Mama must have been nervous too, for they were waiting at the end of the dock to grab the ropes and tie them up.

"I was just about to organize an expedition to go to your rescue," said Papa. "It's getting darkish."

"No rescue needed," Hildy called up happily. "We managed fine all by ourselves."

It had been a blue-ribbon day. Other blue-ribbon days followed, one after another. Hildy had trouble remembering. Which day had they seen what Guy was sure was a kingfisher, and where was it they had found the snapping turtle and the little green lizard? All the sun-filled days ran together.

They regretted the time they had to spend in Arborley helping with the shopping. But Mama said they had to help or they wouldn't eat, and that was important, too, for they all worked up enormous appetites.

Even the posters for the Firemen's Carnival lost their attraction — for everyone except Guy. He still insisted he was going to go, come what may, but the Stuart children were busy thinking about other things.

They explored the other side of the river, but found it uninteresting and full of bugs. The riverbank was low there, but there was no beach, and to secure the boats they had to push them between clumps of tall reeds. After they had gotten their sneakers wet and muddy and were well bitten by mosquitoes, they found the remains of a small dock only a few feet away, hidden by the reeds.

There was a kind of road cut through the trees and they walked along it, squishing and scratching. The trees grew closer together on this side. The bright sunlight filtered through only occasionally. They followed the road for a few minutes until they reached a fork.

"Which one shall we take?" asked Guy, who was in the lead.

"Neither!" said Ellen and Jug promptly, and Ellen added, "There's nothing to see and the bugs are killing me. Let's go back."

"Oh, stop complaining," said Guy, who was scratching, too. "Little kids shouldn't tag along on expeditions if they're going to grouse all the time."

Hildy had been just about to agree with Ellen and Jug

but she closed her mouth quickly. She didn't want to be classed with the little kids.

Without waiting for any more comments Guy took the right fork of the road. It wound through the trees and brush and in a couple of minutes they came into a small clearing. A rickety building leaned crazily against a tree. It had been a stable once, or maybe the start of à summer cottage. Spence unfolded the picture map he was making and tried to figure out where the shed should go.

"Let's see — we left the boats just about opposite our place, and the road curved off like this — sort of — "

It was hard to keep track of the direction when you couldn't see where the sun was.

"It looks as if this road here might go into Arborley," he said. "Arborley should be off in that direction, and not too far, either. The river road winds all around and then crosses the bridge, but this looks as if it goes fairly straight."

"A good quick way to go to the Firemen's Carnival," said Guy. Spence gave him a suspicious look and Guy added, "That is, if anybody was going."

Jug was looking over the shed. "Let's go inside." Spence reached out and caught him by the shirttail.

"And have a piece of the roof fall in on you? Nothing doing! That place is ready to fall any minute."

"The tree is holding it up," Jug argued. But Spence was firm so Jug had to be satisfied with looking in the one cobwebby window. Guy felt like stirring things up that day so he began to talk about haunted houses and deserted cabins in the dark woods.

"Spooky, isn't it? Looks like a real haunted house to me. Aren't you scared?" he said to Hildy. Hildy hadn't

138

thought about it, but all of a sudden it did look spooky.

"Naw, it's just empty," said Jug. "There's nothing in it."

"All haunted houses look empty. In the daytime they look just like this, but at night things begin to move around and you hear groans — " Guy was tugging at the door. It gave way with a scraping noise that sounded loud in the quiet of the woods. They were all startled, even Guy.

Ellen said, "I want to go home," and she moved closer to Hildy for protection.

Nobody cared to go inside and finally Spence said, "Hey, the mosquitoes are really bad! Let's get back to the boats."

At this Guy let out a loud guffaw. "Listen to the big brave Indian chief. Why don't you go inside and check for ghosts?"

"The floorboards might be rotted," said Spence. "People could break a leg falling through a rotted floor. Come on, let's get out of here." They were all glad to hustle out of the clearing and down the narrow road to the river. Guy continued to heckle, but he followed close behind.

"I'll come back here sometime when I don't have a bunch of fraidy-cats along," he said.

They went back to the boats and rowed home. The trip had not been a success, and Guy continued to be annoying. Some days he was so nice that Hildy forgot she had ever objected to his coming to the Roost, and other days — ! Well, this was one of those other days. It was hot, too, muggy and sticky, and even their afternoon swim didn't stop the itching of their mosquito bites.

Guy went on being as itchy as the bug bites, and by bedtime Hildy was saying under her breath, "Go home! Go home! If you don't like it here you can leave!" She knew, though, that the time to ask Guy to leave had passed weeks ago, if ever they were going to do it at all. She also knew that by tomorrow he'd probably be acting all right again. But for tonight, she thought grimly, he'll be lucky if Spence doesn't mangle him. And if Spence does, I'll help.

She amused herself by thinking of all the horrible things they might do to Guy — draw and quarter him, tar and feather him. It took her mind off her bites and off the sultry humid air. Usually she fell asleep the instant her head hit the pillow, but tonight she tossed restlessly.

At sunset they had noticed that heavy thunderhead clouds were piling up, and now and then flashes of far-off heat lightning lit the darkness. There was no breeze and no moon. She heard snatches of angry-sounding whispers from the other side of the porch. Apparently Spence and Guy were no more able to sleep than she was, and were still bickering.

She thought about what Mama had said to her after supper, when they were alone in the kitchen for a few minutes. She and Mama had many such talks — usually on the days when Guy was acting up. Those were the days when Hildy felt most lonely, most out of step. When everything was going well, Guy and Spence accepted her as one of the older ones, a responsible partner in whatever they were planning. But when they were mad at each other, they were mad at everyone and Hildy had better stay away until the air cleared.

Mama said, "Try to understand, Hildy. Imagine how difficult it would be if we Stuarts didn't have each other. We'd be mad at the whole world too. Be patient with the boy. He is improving in so many ways."

Hildy agreed with this. It was true, the bad days were much fewer and farther between than they had been earlier in the summer.

"But what makes him act so awful sometimes? Mean and nasty and complaining about everything!"

Mama sighed. "I wish I knew. It bothers me, too. But try to realize, with his parents making such problems, everything is so hard. With us, living is so much easier."

"Easier? When his folks are rich, and can travel and everything?"

"Yes, easier!" said Mama firmly. "All we are lacking is money, and we can work hard and get that. But that poor child is really poor — no family to take care of him. Of course his grandfather loves him, but it's not the same. Nothing takes the place of a close family like ours. So try to be patient with him."

Hildy thought about this conversation as she turned and tossed and punched her pillow. Even George was hot. Someone on the boys' side tiptoed upstairs, probably to the bathroom, and George moaned a little and then padded up the stairs, breathing heavily. He'd bump down again in a few minutes.

Poor old George. He probably would enjoy a swim. Well, so would I, she thought crossly. I wish we didn't have a rule against it. I'd spend the night on a rock and let the water lap over me.

When Guy was behaving well he obeyed all the rules they had agreed on, and didn't seem to mind. But when he was out of sorts he chafed and strained and fussed, just like George on a leash. More than once Guy had threatened to go for a midnight swim while everyone else was asleep. And once Hildy had a sneaking suspicion he had done it. But it was only a suspicion, and she had no intention of reporting him to Papa unless she had proof.

But then, she thought, we might all be kept out of the water. Papa said . . . She fell asleep before she could finish her thought.

Sometime later, she had no idea how much later — she had a strange dream. She was in a boat, not rowing, just sitting there and moving very fast but silently. It was night in the dream but there was a silvery light from somewhere, enough to see that streamers of fog were blowing past, like long silk banners. They felt deliciously cool against her face. Somewhere there was lively music, calling to her to hurry and join the fun. Then from out of the fog she heard the splash of oars and the sound of a low voice that carried across the water. She rose to her feet and her small dream boat lurched dangerously —

It took a moment for her to realize that the dream was over, that she was awake. She was standing, not in a boat, but on the south porch, and there was no fog, no silvery light. It was as hot and humid as ever and pitch dark. The voices and the splashes were part of the dream too.

She flopped down on her sticky bed and wished for morning to come, and swimming time and —

Was she really awake, or was she dreaming she was awake? Clear as could be she heard the splash of an oar and an exclamation quickly muffled as a boat bumped the dock. She strained to hear, but there was nothing more. The night was full of the usual tiny sounds of buzzing and squeaking and humming and rippling, but nothing more than that. Nothing at all.

I'm cuckoo, she thought. There's no boat out there. Of course there wasn't. Then she heard the dream music again, and all at once everything was as clear as day. That was the sound of a merry-go-round. The Firemen's Carnival! This was the night of the carnival in Arborley, and Guy had sworn he would go, one way or another. So *that* was his scheme — to row across the river, take the narrow road that led from the old shack toward town. He had plenty of money. He could ride on the merry-go-round and eat cotton candy half the night and be back on his mattress sound asleep when everyone awoke the next morning.

How he would laugh at them then! Well, he'd get his. He'd be sent back to Spring Mount in disgrace, and they'd be rid of him for the few days that were left of the summer. No more prima donna airs, no more sulking when he didn't get his own way, no more rubbing it in about his allowance, no more — no more bird lessons, either. And they were just beginning on bugs, too. And wild flowers. She still had a lot to learn.

And then there were the rowing lessons. She did pretty well now, and didn't need him anymore, but at first she couldn't have managed without his help. And once he was convinced she could do it, Guy had helped as much as

Spence in making her learn to swim. Professor Hanley would feel just awful. And it would prove to Guy that no one really wanted him.

She knew then what she had to do. Somehow she had to catch up to Guy and make him come back before anyone else missed him. She wouldn't tell as long as he promised never to do it again. They could finish out the summer without a big hassle that would leave unpleasant memories for everyone. That's what she had to do.

First to make sure that Guy was making the noise she had heard down at the dock. It was just as she suspected. Guy was not on his mattress on the north porch. Jug was snoring and Spence was tossing restlessly in his sleep, but Guy's mattress was empty. Darn him, anyway. Fuming, she fumbled in the dark for her sneakers — the steps and dock were splintery — and with the laces flopping, she hurried down the long flights of stairs as quietly as she could. Her flashlight made only a small pool of light in the surrounding darkness. She hoped if Guy looked back and noticed a flickering light he'd think it was a lightning bug.

She located the *Niña* rocking gently at the end of the dock. *Santa Maria* was there, too — and the *Pinta* was gone! Guy couldn't be too far ahead. It was only minutes since she had heard the splash of his oars.

Up in Guy's room George stirred. He lifted his head and listened, and then with a wild leap that carried him right through the flimsy mosquito netting of the door, he bounded out on the balcony and barked.

Hildy heard him and froze, then pulled on her oars again. Maybe the others heard him, too, but George often barked in the night — at acorns falling on the roof, or cloud shadows drifting across the moon. His bark usually meant nothing, so the sleepers slept on.

Except for one. Guy woke and wished groggily he hadn't got mad at Spence and come upstairs to sleep. It was probably a lot cooler down on the porch. George had torn a hole in the netting again and soon the mosquitoes would find their way in. The foolish dog was barking his head off out on the balcony. "Shut up, dog," he muttered. George was obligingly quiet, and in the quiet Guy could hear the sound of a distant merry-go-round, and nearer — he could have sworn he heard a noise down on the water.

Chapter 15

Aɴᴅ so began the strangest, wildest, most unbelievable night! The next day, when they tried to tell each other what had gone on, it made no sense at all. It was a picture puzzle with the main pieces missing, and no one could tell what the picture was supposed to be.

In the gray light just before sunrise Hildy stood on the dock in her wet canvas shoes, her nightgown mud-stained and bedraggled, her legs and arms scratched, ready to cry with weariness, and tried to remember how it all started.

"I heard a boat," she said, "and I came down here and found that Guy had taken the *Pinta* — "

"That's not true," interrupted Guy. "I was upstairs in bed, and *I* heard a boat — "

"Both the *Pinta* and the *Niña* were gone," said Spence, "and so was Hildy."

"And George barked and barked and me 'n Ellen came

down and everybody was gone and there wasn't a boat left, not any."

"Now you're all back and the *Santa Maria* and the *Pinta* are here —" Papa was confused. "Are you sure you tied up the *Niña*? Tight? Couldn't she have just drifted away and maybe you dreamed all this?"

"No." Hildy was sure of that. "No, because it was the *Niña* I took across the river to find Guy. But coming back it changed into the *Pinta* — I think —"

"Changed into the *Pinta*?"

"I think — I thought so then — but my flashlight was dead. I couldn't see, and I was so scared."

"Just tell me Hildy, *why*? Why would you start off on a pitch-black night to row across the river to find Guy, who was asleep in his bed? Why?"

Hildy couldn't remember now. It all seemed so long ago. "I guess — I didn't want him to get caught."

"Caught at what? And what were you two thinking about, to go after her? If you couldn't find her, why didn't you call us? And what made any of you think — I don't know! I just don't know! With all our safety rules, and you all understood them and agreed they were fair and reasonable — now this! And none of you will even tell me a straight story about what happened!"

"We're trying, Papa, honest. We just don't know what the straight story is." And at last Hildy began to cry.

"Well, now," Mama said, "how about you all get cleaned up and dressed and we'll have a good breakfast, and then maybe things will be clearer."

They washed and dressed and breakfasted and things were no clearer. Not at all. They sat around the kitchen table and worried at the subject, like George with a bone, and got nowhere. Hildy told her story again, patiently, trying to remember every single thing. It was all as confused as ever.

After the morning chores were done, they gathered again at the kitchen table. The storm that had threatened all last night had never come, and it was as hot and sticky as the day before. It was swimming time, but the river was out of bounds now. Papa had said no dock, no water, no boats, and that was that. There was not a chance that he would change his mind. They could hear him pounding away at the typewriter upstairs.

"He's mad as a hornet," said Spence gloomily. "Mad as a yellow jacket."

"And Mama's mad as a carpenter bee," added Ellen. "They're both mad at us, and *we* didn't do anything. Me and Jug, we didn't do anything."

"We did something." Spence was sure of that. "But what was it?"

Hildy remembered something. "Who were those men? First I thought it was you and Gooey, but they had real deep voices."

"There was only one man in that automobile."

"What automobile? These men were going to the dock."

"When? After you rowed across, or what?"

"After. When I was up in the tree."

"Couldn't have been. The auto went back — well, it would have to be toward Arborley, wouldn't it?"

"Get your map. Maybe that'll help."

Spence unfolded the picture map he was making as a record of all the places they had explored during the summer. He had copied the general outlines and the twisting course of the river from a yellowed fly-specked map that hung in the little Arborley post office. Perhaps his map was not terribly accurate, but it was close enough for their purposes. There was the meadow with the boulders, the tree house, the lane that ran out to the main road and their mailbox, the island upstream, and there, across the river from Spence's crazy falling-down drawing of Ramshackle Roost, was the narrow road leading to the shack in the clearing.

They studied the map in silence. Finally Spence said, "If that little road from the shack runs to the east, like this, it wouldn't take more than a few minutes to get to Arborley. Not like taking the river road the long way around where the river bends, and crossing the bridge into town."

"But who would want to row over and go into Arborley that way? You can't get a car over in a rowboat."

"Why would anyone be tramping around in that mosquito jungle, anyway? Especially when they could have been having a good time at the carnival."

"But someone was there. We know that. We saw him and Hildy heard him."

"Them," Hildy corrected Guy. "There were two."

"One or two, it still doesn't make sense."

On the still summer air they could hear the *clip-clop* of Mr. Brown's horse. He was later than usual, and when he rattled up to the back door they found out why. Mr. Brown had an exciting story to tell, and in telling it, he had spent extra time at each house along the way.

Arborley had been robbed! Not just one house, or two,

but practically every single one! When the merry-go-round stopped and the carnival lights were turned off, the good citizens of Arborley went home. Most of them were dead tired and went right to bed without noticing a thing. But a few had — Miss Atwood had never in her life missed brushing her hair one hundred strokes, tired or not tired, and she couldn't find her gold-backed hairbrush. Or the comb, either, or the gold shoehorn that matched. And Mr. Jenkins went to put away his best cuff links, and the little box with the rest of his treasures was gone. He thought he'd mislaid it, or his wife had, and he planned to give her what-for in the morning.

It was early in the morning that the news started to get around. There was hardly a household where something wasn't missing. All small things — good jewelry, silver picture frames, silver cream pitchers, sugar bowls. Amos Mellerman's valuable stamp collection, too — almost broke his heart, that did. And Bill Pryor's grandfather's watch and chain. And Mrs. Pettinghill, who didn't trust banks, and everybody knew she kept her savings under the mattress. The list went on and on.

"You didn't miss nothin' here?" Mr. Brown asked. "Well, I reckon them robbers figured people weren't bringing valuables to a summer place. Anyways, they cleaned out Arborley, they sure did. Clean as a whistle, and them thieves picked the right night for it. Firemen's Carnival night."

He filled the icebox and hurried away to the next stop, and the next audience. Nobody said a word until the sound of the horse and wagon faded away through the trees. Then Spence said thoughtfully, "Do you sup-

pose — ? What if the sounds we heard, and the men —
did it all have anything to do with the robbery?"

"Spence," said Hildy eagerly, "let's be scientific. Let's
start at the very beginning and you make a diagram and
we'll trace every move. We'll see where we all were when
the others were somewhere else, and if those were the
robbers, where they must have been when all of us were
where we were — "

It was very confusing, but Spence got the idea. He
made a rough approximation of the curving river and located Arborley, the shack and dock at Ramshackle Roost.

"Now! Let's start with all of us in bed, and the three
boats tied up at the dock. I know we tied them — the
Pinta didn't just drift away. So here are the boats. But
when Hildy went down to the dock the Pinta was gone,
and we don't know where."

"Show a dotted line out into the river," suggested Guy,
"so if later we figure it out you can put it in."

They marked the path of the Niña across the river and
into the reeds where Hildy had pushed it. That left only
the Santa Maria at the dock, and Spence and Guy took
that across. They saw the Niña in the reeds and pulled up
close alongside.

Already the map was a jumble of lines. The diagram
was a mess. Spence started all over again. The second
time it was neater, but not really clearer. He tried a line
made up of arrows to show their comings and goings in the
boats, footprints to show where they walked, dotted lines
to show where they weren't sure.

"Forget the lines, Spence. That's only making it worse.
Markers! That's what we need. Markers!"

151

Hildy and Jug got the idea at the same time and raced to find the tiddlywinks they knew were stuck away in a drawer somewhere. There were three broken sets, but altogether it made an imposing pile of markers.

"Red for the *Santa Maria*, green for *Pinta*, blue for *Niña*. The big ones will be boats — and here, a big yellow one for the car. And we'll be the little ones so we can ride in the boats — matching colors for the regular crews."

Jug and Ellen insisted on markers for themselves and their parents, even though they had gone only down the steps to the dock. A brown button was fine for George.

Spence said excitedly, "At each change of position, I'll write it down like a sailor's logbook, and we'll move the markers, and then it will be as clear as crystal."

It wasn't that simple, but the markers helped. They had a pile of scrap paper — leftovers from Papa's wastebasket — and so they began again.

The first entry in the log was easy. The three boats were lined up at the dock, red, green and blue. The small markers were on the porch except for Papa's and Mama's and Guy's and George's. They were on the second floor. Step number 2 was not so easy. From somewhere, someone had come and rowed away in the *Pinta*.

"For now, we'll just guess it was the robbers and put it across the river."

"But if the robbers were busy in Arborley, what were they doing rowing around in the dark?"

It was an interesting question, and one for which they had no answer. They wrote the question in the log to be answered later, they hoped, and went on to number 3. Hildy had awakened to the sound of oars, checked on

Guy's porch bed and found it empty, assumed he was gone. She went down to the dock. The *Pinta* was missing and that made her sure he was rowing across the river. So she got into the *Niña* — Spence put Hildy's blue marker on top of the blue boat marker — and rowed to the other side.

Guy was mystified at all this. "I don't get it," he said, shaking his head. "Why didn't you guess I got sore and went upstairs to sleep? Why would you think I'd go out in the *Pinta* at night?"

"Because it was the carnival night. And, well, sometimes I thought you went swimming at night — "

He flushed right up to the roots of his sun-bleached hair. "Once. Once I was mad, and I went. But I felt so lousy about cheating, I didn't have much fun. But what made you come after me? You could've just told on me."

It was Hildy's turn to be embarrassed. "You'd be sent home," she mumbled. "It seemed like a bad end to a pretty good summer. I thought I'd catch up to you and make you come back."

"Well!" Spence was astonished. "Old cowardy-custard Hildy! You really got brave!" He wasn't being sarcastic. He meant it. Jug and Ellen were staring at her with real admiration.

"I couldn't've. I never, never would have done it," said Ellen. And Jug said, "Wow!"

Hildy thought back over the dark sticky frightening night before and scratched thoughtfully at a mosquito bite. "I don't think I'd do it again. I'm not that brave," she said modestly. "First I was too busy catching up to Gooey — well, I thought that was what I was doing, anyway — and I didn't have time to be scared. But after, in that tree, and

those men and everything — I've never been so scared."
She shivered, and said hastily, "Let's get on with number
four."

"Where did you leave the *Niña?*"

"I tried to head for that broken-down dock so I could tie
her up but I missed it. I ran her into a mess of high grass
and reeds, deep enough so I knew she wouldn't float out.
I splashed around in the water and mud until I came to
solid ground and it was the road. I could see those tree
stumps that we noticed before. My flashlight was working
fine then. I went as fast as I could to catch up to Gooey,
but I didn't, and when I came to the place where the road
forks, I didn't know which way to go. I called — that's
when I got scared. Boy, was it *awful!* I was so sure he
was just ahead of me and would answer. There wasn't a
sound, just me. I shone my light all around and the trees
were so tall and black. I was so scared I was afraid to turn
around and run back to the boat and I was afraid to go on."

"Wow!" said Jug again, very respectfully.

"Then I got so scared I got mad. I was mad enough to
tear Gooey limb from limb. I could've peeled him like a
banana, honest. So I climbed that tree at the fork of the
road — you remember, the branches came down pretty
close and we sort of ducked to get under? — and I decided
I'd wait all night if I had to, but when he came by I'd
jump down and scare him so bad he'd never forget it."
She paused for breath.

"Gee! What then?"

"I — I went to sleep."

It was such an anticlimax that everyone laughed.

Chapter 16

THEY WERE LAUGHING when Mama came into the kitchen.

"It's nice that you are all feeling so funny," she said huffily. "Your father and I didn't think last night was such a joke. Now clear off the table. We'll be eating soon."

"Oh, Mama, we're almost finished."

"I'd say you were completely finished. The only way you could be more finished would be to be sent back to Spring Mount."

Spence said, "Heck, Mama, you don't have to rub it in. We weren't laughing because we thought last night was funny, honest." Spence could almost always talk Mama out of it when she was mad. "We're trying to solve the mystery. Give us a couple of minutes more and we'll clean up."

She nodded, but they could tell by the way she slammed the icebox door that she was plenty sore. They hurried to

155

step number 4 and put Hildy in the tree at the fork of the two roads. Then came number 5. It was going on at the same time as 3 and 4, but there was no way to show that, so they just left the Hildy marker in the tree and went back to Ramshackle Roost, back to the point where George barked and broke through the mosquito netting in Guy's room. He barked and barked and Guy awakened, sweaty and sticky and cross.

"I was wishing I was downstairs on the porch where at least I'd be a little bit cooler. So when George wouldn't shut up and go back to sleep, I decided I'd let him out and sneak back out to my mattress on the porch."

Guy went as far as the porch and let George out the screen door so he wouldn't lean on it and tear another hole. George went hurrying down the steps to the dock, as if he might be chasing something, and just because he was so hot and cross, Guy followed.

"I thought I'd sit on the dock and cool my feet. I swear I didn't plan to go in the water."

On the dock, in a quiet moment between barks, Guy heard something, a splash. It could have been a fish jumping, but then he heard another splash and the squeak of an oarlock. And that was no fish.

"I tried not to splash," said Hildy.

"It was too dark to see, but I could feel. I felt along the dock and I found one boat tied up. I pawed all over those splintery posts but I couldn't find any more. There was only one boat there, I was sure of it."

George had finally given up barking and galumphed off into the bushes after some little night animal. Guy gave up the search for the other boats and hurried up the steps

156

again. Something was going on, he felt sure of it, and whatever it was, he had been left out.

Spence moved the Guy marker back up to the porch and wrote:

Question: Who was splashing?

Answer: Probably Hildy.

Question: If it was Hildy, where was the third boat?

Answer: ?

Mama was pouring milk now, and looking as if she wanted to set the table, so they speeded up. Guy continued, "I never even thought about Hildy. I was sure I'd find Spence's bed empty."

"Scared me out of a year's growth," grumbled Spence. "When you patted my face and shook me, I thought it was the end of the world."

"So did I," said Guy. "Because if it wasn't you out in that boat, then who was it?"

"I don't know why nobody thought it was me," Jug complained. "You all acted as if I wasn't alive. If it hadn't been for George barking so much later on, me'n Ellen would have missed everything."

"Me'n Papa would have, too," Mama was muttering in the background. "Hurry up, there. It's getting on for noon."

"Wait!" pleaded Spence, talking faster and whipping two markers down the steps to the dock. "We checked, and Hildy was gone, and then we were really scared. Two boats missing, Hildy gone, Jug and Ellen sound asleep. Guy was sure the rowing noise came from directly opposite, not upstream or down, so that's the way we went. We didn't know what else to do."

Mama said, "Never occurred to you to call your parents! Never the direct sensible way. Oh, no!"

"We didn't think we had time. We rowed as fast as we could, didn't even worry about being quiet. We just wanted to find Hildy. We headed for the dock and missed it. We saw the *Niña* jammed into the reeds and knew we were on her trail. Then Guy flashed his light around and we saw the dock so we started to tie up there, and on the other side of the dock, there was the *Pinta* and another rowboat — right here. Hand me a black button, Jug, for the other boat."

Question: If Hildy rowed over in the *Niña*, how did the *Pinta* get there? And where did the other boat come from?

Answer: ?

"It looked fishy to me," said Guy, "and I was mad because someone took the *Pinta*, so I shoved her under the dock, and the *Santa Maria*, too. You could've seen them easy enough in the daylight, I guess, but it was pretty dark over there under the trees, even with a flashlight."

They turned off their lights and went as silently as they could along the narrow road. There was something very wrong about the whole situation, and it seemed very important now to be quiet until they found out what was going on. The sound of the merry-go-round was closer on this side of the river. Evidently they were not far at all from Arborley.

"Where were you, Hildy? Were you still in the tree? Why didn't you say anything when we went by?"

"I was scared. I woke up with a jump and I saw the

158

light flash on and off and I didn't know where I was for a minute, and by that time it was dark again and whoever it was had gone, but it sounded like two people. So I sat there and shook because I thought if it was Guy he'd be coming from the other direction, see? So maybe it wasn't Guy. I sat there for a long time trying to make up my mind what to do. By this time I didn't care if I caught up to Guy or scared him or anything. I just wanted to go home. While I was getting up my nerve to climb down and run, I heard someone coming from the other direction. I heard voices and I saw the lights — they weren't bothering about being quiet at all. I hung on to the branch and hoped the leaves were thick enough to hide me. They would've seen me in a minute if they'd flashed the lights up. I was so close I was right over their heads. Oh glory be, I was shaking. Each one had a big sack on his shoulder — "

There wasn't a sound in the kitchen. Even Mama, who had been rattling around making sandwiches, was quiet as a mouse.

"The robbers!" whispered Jug.

"Robbers?" Mama yelled. "Robbers? What robbers?"

"The robbers who robbed every house in Arborley last night while the carnival was going on."

"And you were up in a tree right over their heads, Hildy?" Now Mama was so excited she was screeching. "In the *woods, alone,* at *night?* Where were you, Spence? Why weren't you keeping an eye on your little sister?"

"Me'n Ellen would've been glad to," Jug offered helpfully, "but nobody woke us up."

159

Guy and Spence looked at each other. "It's beginning to fall into place," said Spence solemnly. He moved markers and wrote, then read aloud,

"Question: What was in the sacks?

"Answer: Most of Arborley.

"Now here's Hildy still in the tree, and here are the two robbers going to the boat."

"Boats," said Guy. "Their boat and the *Pinta*."

"Their boat and the *Niña*," corrected Hildy. "When I got back to the dock after they made their second trip" — Spence wrote the second trip on his chart — "the *Niña* was gone. I guess they couldn't find the *Pinta* and took *Niña* instead."

Mama grabbed the dinner bell and began to ring it frantically. "I want your father here to listen to this!" she shouted over the loud clang. "I want him to hear the whole awful story! Robbers! Thieves! And you children running around in the dark with a bunch of cutthroats!"

Spence tried to say, "They didn't cut any throats — " but he was drowned out by the bell. Papa came down the steps on the run. This wasn't the usual summons to lunch, and he knew it. Mama was still ringing when he skidded to a stop in the kitchen.

For a short while it was bedlam with everyone yelling and Papa not understanding a word. He finally got the bell away from Mama and made her sit down. He pounded on the table for quiet. When things were quiet he said, "You're all here so no one has drowned or fallen from a tree or anything. Will you please tell me what's going on?"

The gabbling broke out again, and he roared, "Silence!"

Then in his gentlest voice he pleaded, "Spencer, as the oldest of my children, will you tell me what in heaven's name is going on here? Or have the whole bunch of you gone stark raving crazy? Tell me, Spence — not you, Sara, you're nutty as a fruitcake," he added to Mama who had opened her mouth to speak.

She closed it quickly as Spence said, "We're on the track of something serious, and we've got it almost figured out. There are just a few clues missing."

Starting with Mr. Brown's account of the robberies in Arborley, so Papa would know from the beginning what the mystery was, Spence read from the logbook as Guy moved the markers on the map. Papa was fascinated. The author in him took over from the irate parent, and he seemed to forget that it was his children and his friend's grandchild who were blundering around in the woods across the river. He was just paying attention to the story with only an occasional question whenever a point wasn't quite clear.

Mama hadn't forgotten she was a mother, and every so often she started to get excited again. Papa patted her back gently to calm her down, and the story went on without interruption. He was so engrossed that he didn't notice the sound of tires on gravel, but Mama did. She flew to the window and gasped.

"It's Professor Hanley and — oh, no, I can't believe it!"

It was. The Conrad ladies, beaded bags and all. Professor Hanley was helping Miss Ida down from his car, and Miss Emma was marching in, sort of grim and sour as usual.

"Look who's here!" Professor Hanley announced. "I

met your good neighbors at church this morning and they agreed to a spin in my motor car and a visit here."

With all the excitement that morning the Stuarts had forgotten that it was Sunday and that Professor Hanley would be arriving as usual. And of course a visit with the Conrad ladies was nothing they were expecting at all — ever.

Mama smoothed her apron and her hair and was out in a flash, standing hospitably on the doorstep and welcoming the guests. From the slightly dazed look on her face Hildy guessed she was counting heads and wondering if Sunday dinner would stretch, and if, by any chance, it would appeal to such picky eaters as Miss Emma and Miss Ida.

Papa was so excited about the mystery and the logbook that he wasted no time on pleasantries.

"You'll never believe what's been going on in the quiet little town of Arborley. Reads like a novel, except that we haven't figured out the ending. Look here!"

They all crowded around the table as Papa said, "Let's start from the beginning, Spence. Maybe Professor Hanley and the ladies will have some suggestions."

"Now, Paul," Mama said firmly. "I really will need the table for lunch." Then she added uncertainly, looking at Miss Emma and Miss Ida, "We usually have just peanut butter sandwiches for lunch, but if you'll tell me what you can eat, I'll be glad to fix it."

"Well, of course, we never eat sandwiches," began Miss Emma, "but perhaps poached eggs — "

The ride in Professor Hanley's auto must have gone to Miss Ida's head, for she said:

"Poached eggs for you if you like, Emma. I'll have a peanut butter sandwich. I haven't had one for years. And why bother to set the table, Mrs. Stuart? Can't we just hold our sandwiches in our hands?"

Miss Emma looked at her sister as if she had suddenly gone mad, but Miss Ida went on cheerfully:

"Now, please, tell us about the mystery. There's nothing so exciting as a good unsolved mystery."

Mama began to laugh at Miss Emma's expression and quickly turned the laugh to a cough that she smothered in her apron. She bustled around making more sandwiches and putting the poached eggs on to cook. After a moment, Miss Emma decided to join the group at the table, and in no time at all she was as engrossed in the story as the rest of them.

Spence began at the beginning and explained about the Firemen's Carnival in Arborley, and where they all were at bedtime on Saturday evening. Professor Hanley raised his bushy white eyebrows when Spence said, "Gooey decided to sleep upstairs in his bedroom."

Guy said cheerfully, "It's all right, Grandfather, I was a sorehead and Spence and I had a fight, but it's all right now."

"It wasn't our first fight and it probably won't be our last," added Spence matter-of-factly. Professor Hanley had a very odd look on his face, both pleased and surprised. His grandson was being treated like one of the family, and that, after all, was what he had hoped would happen.

Chapter 17

S o far it all checks out," said Papa. "Thieves choose the one time when everyone in town will be away from home, rob everybody blind and no one notices until hours later. But why thrash around in the woods? What sense does that make?"

There was a long silence while everyone thought, and then Miss Ida said timidly, "Of course, I'm no expert on crime, but it seems to me — well, the automobile the boys saw in the woods is an important clue, I think."

"Nonsense, Ida." Her sister was businesslike and brisk. "If the automobile had anything to do with the crime, the robbers would have been riding away in it, it stands to reason. It was merely someone out for a cooling ride, without a doubt."

Miss Ida was not entirely convinced. "Still, it bothers me — "

They mulled it over for a while, but it really didn't fit

in, that automobile parked on the bumpy road to Arborley. Why would anyone take a cooling ride into dense woods, filled with mosquitoes, on a road so full of stones and ruts they could only creep along? Unless —

"Unless," said Hildy suddenly, "they only borrowed the car for a short while, to get the loot into the woods, and had to get it back to town before anyone noticed it was gone."

"No one in the world would notice that a rowboat was gone, though." Papa was beginning to catch fire. "They could row away and hide the stuff and sell it later!"

"And they discovered they had stolen too much to fit into one boat, so they rowed across in their boat and took ours."

The platter of sandwiches was empty and Mama got up to make some more. Detecting made everyone hungry. Miss Ida munched dreamily, like a large placid cow chewing her cud. She evidently was enjoying her peanut butter sandwich, but her mind was not on lunch.

"I keep coming back to the automobile," she said. "I read so many mysteries to help me fall asleep," she added apologetically, "and you know, they never put in a clue that doesn't turn out to mean *something* — "

"But that's in a story," said Papa. "In real life there must be all sorts of clues that turn out to mean nothing at all."

She nodded and munched some more.

"If the automobile was stolen too — " Wheels were beginning to turn in Hildy's mind and she began to talk faster and faster. "Suppose the automobile was stolen just for the evening — suppose the thief borrowed it, maybe, knowing the family'd be at the carnival, and he could unload it and get it back and show up at the carnival and make sure everyone saw him there — they do that in detective stories," she said, "and it throws everyone off the track."

"Suppose the other thief had been at the carnival early so nobody would suspect him either," added Miss Ida. "In that case they'd be local people that everyone would recognize."

"Wait a minute! Didn't Mr. Brown tell us once that Hilltown had been cleaned out too, just about the first day we came here? Could it have been the same ones?"

It seemed as if it could, but the trail ended there. They couldn't think of another clue that led anywhere.

"Just like in a book," said Miss Ida. "The trail leads to the water, boats don't leave a trace behind, bloodhounds can't follow the scent, thieves vanish into thin air. Just exactly like a book."

"It seems to me, Sister Ida," Miss Emma said sharply, "you must have been wasting a lot of your time reading trashy fiction. I read myself to sleep with more uplifting literature."

"What kind of motor car was it?" asked Professor Hanley hastily to change the subject. "It shouldn't be too hard to trace in a small town like Arborley."

It had been too dark to tell. Spence and Guy tried to remember, but the car had been only a black shape on a pitch-black road. And with the men coming and going with their bags, the boys had stayed crouched behind a bush, not daring to move. All they were sure of was that two men had carried the bags along the road to the river, and one had backed the car slowly out in the direction of Arborley.

Hildy had been doodling idly on a piece of paper. She doodled 1 automobile, 2 boats, 3 robbers, 4 what? Nothing. 1 automobile, 2 boats, 3 robbers — it was like a counting rhyme. 1 auto, 2 — why two boats? If the bags of loot were to be hidden nearby, why take the time and the risk of stealing another rowboat from clear across the river? Why not two trips in their own boat? Did that mean a long trip, then? Where to? And wouldn't two loaded rowboats be noticed somewhere along the way?

"Not if they were fishing," she said aloud. Her remark didn't make sense to the others. They were still thinking about the automobile in the dark. She explained, and added, "Even if someone happened to be out at night or early morning, nobody'd think twice about a couple of fishermen out on the river."

The rest of them still didn't get the connection, so she went back a little and explained, "They could float down the river to a sizable town — would that be Spring Mount? — and sell the stuff."

"I believe," said Miss Ida excitedly, "I do believe Hildy has hit on the answer. And I think the thieves lived in Arborley or Hilltown or somewhere in between because they knew the town habits so well, and if Hildy is right, two of them should be well on the way to Spring Mount right now."

"Then there is no time to lose," said Professor Hanley, sounding exactly like a detective story. "We'll drive into Arborley and tell the Constable and he can telephone Spring Mount! Hurry!"

They dashed for the back door, Spence clutching the chart and Guy with a handful of markers. They saw at once that all of them couldn't go. There just wasn't room. So Mama tied her apron back on and made the supreme sacrifice. "I'll stay here," she said bravely. "Tell me all about it."

Miss Ida and Miss Emma said together, "I'll stay here, of course," but Jug settled that one.

"Miss Ida should come because she helped solve the mystery, and me'n Ellen *hafta* because we missed all the rest of the fun, and Spence and Gooey can stay here."

Spence and Guy were already shoving into the back seat and did not intend to be left behind. And at the last moment George decided to go too. With a tremendous leap he vaulted into the back of the car and sat sprawled across all the laps, panting and drooling slightly.

Professor Hanley was very proud of his touring car and under ordinary circumstances George would have been shoved out again. But Papa had already turned the crank and the Professor had the motor roaring. There was only time for Papa to leap into the front and slam the door, and they were off down the lane in a shower of gravel.

Now that the mystery had been solved, and only the small matter of catching the robbers was left, they all felt that speed was essential. Professor Hanley urged his auto on with encouraging remarks, "Come on, old girl! Show us the stuff you're made of!" Hildy had never gone so fast in all her life. The wind whipped her hair and flapped her middy collar. It was quite different from their usual trips into Arborley with Mr. Brown and his ice wagon.

It was all very thrilling, but no one was paying much attention to the scenery that flashed past. Except George. He leaned into the breeze and let it tumble his frowzy curls, and never missed a thing on either side of the road. George was a born automobilist, and he was just then finding it out.

Arborley seemed deserted — it was Sunday dinner hour and everyone was inside. They realized then that they didn't know the Constable's name or his address and there was no one around to ask. After their mad dash into town it was frustrating to cruise slowly down the main street and not see a soul.

Finally they spotted a man on his front lawn, taking a nap under a tree.

"Oh dear," said Miss Ida. "Should we disturb his sleep?"

"We have no choice." Professor Hanley was firm. "Too much is at stake! Hallooo, there," he bellowed. It was so unexpected that everyone in the car jumped. So did the sleeping man. "The Constable! Where can we find the Constable, or the Sheriff — or the Chief of Police?"

"Down the street, three houses, green shutters — " the man called sleepily, and then yelled after them, "Speed-crazy fools!"

That the Constable was not too glad to see them was not surprising. They were, after all, a very odd-looking group. The Professor and Miss Ida had started out properly dressed, but by now they were wind-tossed and messy-looking. And the rest of them had not been done up for a Sunday visit to begin with. Hildy tried to pull up her drooping bloomer leg and pull down her unironed middy. It was the first time she had thought about clothes since they left Spring Mount.

The Constable's wife eyed them suspiciously, but agreed to call her husband from his dinner. They could smell chicken and gravy, and it smelled good.

"Come in, I guess," Constable Adams said crossly. "What's this all about, that has to be taken care of right this minute?"

They all started to speak at once, but Professor Hanley motioned to Papa, and he did the talking for the group. The suspicious look on the Constable's face grew even more noticeable as Papa explained. This was something they had not counted on at all — that their story would not be believed.

"Don't you see?" Papa asked desperately. "It's all so clear."

"Don't see nothin' worth missing good chicken dumplings for," he grumbled. "Sounds like a pack of nonsense thought up by overheated city people. You're that writer fellow, aren't you?"

"Yes, but this isn't made up. Think about it," Papa urged. "See how it all fits together."

"Fits together like a bunch of gibble-gabble. Bunch of kids go out in the boats and don't tie them up right and blame it on the robbers. Sounds like a fish story to me. Write it down, young man, and put it in a book and them as don't understand the workings of the Law'll believe every word of it. But not me."

He turned to go back to his waiting dinner.

170

"Wait!" the Professor roared. He was really a good roarer, Hildy noted with satisfaction. Mr. Adams spun around, his face red as a beet. But Professor Hanley didn't give him a chance.

"I *demand* that you telephone to the Chief of Police in Spring Mount and alert him that the thieves may be on their way! If you do not, sir, I myself will apprehend the robbers and make a citizen's arrest! And then I will report that you refused to do your duty!"

"Now, wait," sputtered Mr. Adams. "You got no call to come bustin' in like this demandin' nothing!"

"Which will it be, sir?" the Professor's usually gentle voice boomed out. "Will you do it, or must I?"

Mr. Adams wilted under the blast. He shrugged his shoulders and went toward the kitchen to phone. Professor Hanley and Papa followed close behind, and the rest of the motley crew were going to tag along, but Mr. Adams said, "The rest of you, wait outside. We don't need you tracking up the clean floor. And get that dog outta my petunias!"

They hurried to obey. George had tired of waiting in the back seat and was resting in an old rowboat filled with pink petunias that ornamented Constable Adams' front yard. The petunias were pretty crushed, but with a bit of rearranging and fluffing up, they didn't look too awful. Hildy hoped they could get away before Mr. Adams looked at them too closely.

The ride home was not nearly so exciting. Not nearly so fast, either, for Professor Hanley drove carefully this time. George was the only one who seemed to enjoy the

trip. The rest of them had little to say, but each one was busy thinking, "Was it all gibble-gabble? Did we make it up and get worked up over nothing?"

The rain that had threatened all the evening before finally arrived in great pelting drops that soaked Guy and Spence before they could get all the rain curtains buttoned on. They arrived home damp and discouraged.

Mama and Miss Emma were waiting for them. Mama seemed pathetically glad to see them, as if they had been gone for days. Evidently visiting with Miss Emma had been hard going. She didn't melt as easily as Miss Ida did, that was plain.

"No doubt about it," Mama said briskly. "What you all need is a good nourishing meal. It's all ready. I'll have it browned in a jiffy."

"Not on that stove, you won't," Miss Emma said. "The

kindling is laid all the wrong way, and the draft is wrong. Let me show you the right way to do it."

The Monster was Mama's baby. She was the one person who could get a fire going in it and keep it going, and she was proud of it. And here was old snippy Miss Emma bossing her around just the way she bossed Miss Ida. From the sudden flash in Mama's eyes, Hildy thought there was going to be trouble, but Mama swallowed hard and said meekly, "Well, if you insist — "

Miss Emma did insist, and she poked and rattled around until she had a nice fire burning, no better than Mama's. She was very pleased with herself.

"There," she said. "It takes a special knack, and I've got it."

Maybe her triumph over the stove helped, or her curiosity about their trip to Arborley, but whatever it was, Miss Emma unbent just a trifle and decided she would try just a taste of the big chicken pie that Mama took out of the oven. She helped herself to a good-sized taste, too. Her plate was just as full as anyone else's.

The rain was shut outside; the kitchen was warm and bright with the light of the oil lamp. Their dinner smelled three times as good as Constable Adams' had, and suddenly the world seemed like not such a bad place after all.

Chapter 18

JUG REFUSED to be comforted by the warmth and the light and the good dinner.

"I've lost my appetite," he announced after he had cleaned up his second helping of chicken pie. "That mean old Mr. Adams was *terrible* — he spoiled the whole summer!"

"Yeah," agreed Ellen, with her mouth full, "he spoiled the whole summer, all right. He wrecked it."

"Oh, for heaven's sake, kids, he only spoiled a little bit of it." Spence had cheered up considerably. "The worst part is we'll never know how the mystery turned out. We'll always wonder if our detecting was right, and there's no way to find out. But the rest of the summer was pretty good."

"I don't care," insisted Ellen. "I'd like to catch that mean old Mr. Adams and — and — I'd punch him right in the belly!"

"Ellen!"

"Well, I would, Mama. I was going to go back to school and tell everybody how we detected and caught the bad men, and now — yah!"

Hildy had thought of that, too, on the way into Arborley. It would give her something very special to write about on the first English assignment. "What I Did on My Vacation." No one, not one other person in the sixth grade would be able to write about catching robbers. Hildy had thought it would help her over that first hard day of school.

"I'm sorry this detecting business ever came up," Mama said. "Now we'll always be a little dissatisfied and wondering. It makes the summer feel like a failure, when really it has been wonderful."

"How was it so wonderful?" Jug was still gloomy.

"Well, for one thing, you had your tree house and the stone stores — "

"Yeah," he agreed, brightening. "And Hildy learned to swim."

"And all the rest of us got much better at it — yes, I did too, don't you laugh!"

They all had to laugh at Mama. Her swimming style had stayed exactly the same — the funny old-fashioned breast stroke that kept her head high out of the water while she lunged along like a playful hippo. But it was true about the rest of them. They all felt completely at home in the water and in the boats, too. It would be hard to leave the three — no, only two now — rowboats behind when they went back to Spring Mount.

And the space! They had roamed all over with no walls

or streets to hem them in. Hildy thought about all the things she had learned from Guy, and said, before she thought:

"I know a meadowlark from a chickadee, and I can recognize a million plants and trees, thanks to Gooey."

Guy grinned and seemed really pleased that she had mentioned it. He had forgotten, apparently, that he told her never to mention it. But that had been a long while ago.

Professor Hanley was wiping his glasses, which had gotten all steamy. His eyes seemed to be watering slightly.

"I think Gooey and I owe a lot to this summer at Ramshackle Roost." His voice cracked and he polished and polished his spectacles. Hildy realized that he had called his grandson Gooey, the first time he had used the nickname that made him wince only a few weeks ago.

"Well, Gooey helped us a lot besides the birds and plants. He knew how to patch a boat and how to row, and now we all know."

"And Paul, your book is almost finished, and it's going to be great, and *I* never had such a relaxing summer in my life," Mama said.

All during the meal, George had been lying by the stove, but now he decided to make the rounds of the table hoping that someone would slip him a treat. He rose suddenly by Miss Emma's side and offered to shake hands. She gave a little scream of surprise, and said, as usual, "Get down! Get down, you — beast!" when Miss Ida interrupted.

"Nonsense, Emma, all he wants to do is be friendly." She leaned across her sister and shook George's paw warmly. "He's a simply magnificent dog, he has real understanding. Just look at the way he knew to roll on Constable Adams' petunias. Go on, shake his hand, sister," Miss Ida urged.

"Well — " Reluctantly Miss Emma took George's big paw and gave it a quick gingerly shake.

Wonders will never cease, thought Hildy. Mama and George together have won over the Conrad ladies at least a little. It was just one more good thing that had come out of the summer at Ramshackle Roost.

"We're getting awfully soupy and sentimental," said Papa, clearing his throat. "The sun's trying to get out. Let's all help with the dishes and see about a swim."

Nothing, not one word was said about the early morning rule of NO WATER! NO BOATS! NO DOCK! It was as if the sun struggling to get through the clouds was wiping out the whole crazy robbery adventure. Maybe they had dreamed it all, anyway. It didn't seem to matter.

They cleared the table in a flash and put away the leftovers for later. Miss Ida marveled at the size of the icebox, and Miss Emma said grudgingly that the stove was fine if it was handled correctly. She still insisted that Mama was wrong on the stove draft, but she wasn't quite as sharp and sour as usual.

Even Professor Hanley took a dish towel and helped dry, though he didn't do it very expertly. Hildy had to give each damp plate an extra swipe or two before she put it away. It was absolutely the jolliest dish-washing they had ever had, and everyone was so busy talking and laughing that at first they didn't notice the sound of a motor car in the lane.

George did, of course, and flung himself against the screen door with a booming bark of welcome. The latch gave way and he crashed outside. One of the two men standing there was Mr. Brown, the iceman. Experienced by now, he stepped quickly out of George's impetuous way. But the other — oh gracious, it was Constable Adams — was caught unaware and off balance. Before the Constable had struggled to his feet and before Papa had pulled George away the happy animal had managed to get in at least one wet slobbery kiss!

"Oh, heaven help us!" moaned Mama. "It's jail for all of us now!"

But it wasn't jail at all, it turned out. When the officer of the law had been brushed off and had been apologized to by everyone, even Ellen, he had some apologizing to do himself.

"It seemed only fair to tell you," he explained, keeping a nervous eye on George all the while, "that you were right after all. The thieves were on their way to Spring Mount, and the Sheriff caught 'em red-handed."

"And the whole town is in your debt, the whole bloomin' town. Miss Atwood'll get back her gold hairbrush, and Amos Mellerman his stamp collection and Mrs. Pettingill her money. You never seen so many grateful people in your life as there were in Arborley when the news got out. Yessir! They sure are grateful and — "

"Hush, Henry." Mr. Adams wanted to tell the story but Mr. Brown enjoyed news too much to be hushed.

"And when the Constable, here, said he wasn't even

sure just where you folks lived, I said you can ask Henry Brown where anyone in this whole area lives and he can lead you there blindfolded, yessir, blindfolded — "

"Should've been gagged, too," muttered Constable Adams, but Mr. Brown rushed happily on.

"So I said, wind up your auto, Constable, I'm your man, I'll show you the way and put in a word or two so that nice family will know how much the citizens of Arborley appreciate people who are brave and daring and straight-thinking enough to figure out a crime like this — "

"I guess the Law could've figured it out, Henry, given the facts and a little time to consider. You got to admit," he said to Papa, "you surely got to admit that it sounded unlikely the first time around."

The Stuarts were not paying too much attention to either Mr. Brown or Mr. Adams. They were yelling and hugging one another and the Hanleys and the Conrads, and George was leaping and barking and kissing. It was bedlam! Mama was the first one to pull herself together and remember her manners.

"It was kind of you and Mr. Brown to motor all the way out here to tell us," she said. "Do come in, both of you, and we'll have iced tea on the front porch and you can give us all the details."

They accepted with pleasure for, as Constable Adams explained, there were a good many confusing points to straighten out and put down on paper for his full report to the Sheriff of Morgan County.

It was almost dark by the time the last question was hashed over and written down. Constable Adams turned out to be not such a bad person after all, generous in his praise of their clever detecting and very sorry that he had doubted their story in the first place.

"Not at all." Papa was inclined to be generous, too. "It was a most unusual kind of tale. We were confused ourselves when Hildy first explained it."

"You've got a remarkably courageous daughter there, Mr. Stuart. That Hildy's got real cool nerve under fire. We need more people like that in the Law, yessirree bob! Any time you want a job, young lady, just let me know. And you can be sure all this'll be in the paper. The man from the *Courier* will be out in the morning."

"Paper only comes out once a week," explained Mr. Brown, who just loved to explain. "Not like them city daily papers, but believe me, we read every word of it. The name of Hildy Stuart will go down in Arborley history, and all the rest of you, too."

They finally drove off, Constable Adams to write his report, and Mr. Brown to spread the news firsthand.

"The ice will be hours late tomorrow," sighed Mama. "Mr. Brown will have a long stop at every house." But it was a happy sigh. The summer at Ramshackle Roost was drawing to a very satisfactory end.

Hildy could hardly believe it — she, Hildy Stuart, was going to be in the Arborley *Courier!* A courageous heroine, a detective with nerves of steel under fire! She thought of how she had sat in the tree and shivered, scared to stay and scared to come down. It would make a good composition on the first day of school.

Suddenly Professor Hanley realized how late it was.

"Come, ladies, we must get on the road before it gets

fully dark," he said, "although I hate to leave. It has been a most satisfying visit. I can't remember when I've had such a good time."

The Conrad ladies agreed. Miss Emma was still nervous around George, but Miss Ida shook his paw in farewell and let him kiss her cheek.

Professor Hanley put his arm around his grandson. "I'll be back to pick you up next Sunday. In the meantime, make the most of this last week. Say," he noticed, "look how you've grown! You're a lot taller than when you came!"

"And a *whole lot* nicer," added Jug loudly, with his usual tact. There was an instant's embarrassed pause while the Stuarts tried to think how to cover that one up. Spence thought quickest and said, "You know, we all are. Taller and nicer."

"Can't ask more of a summer than that, can you? Taller and nicer both?" That was Papa.

"And healthier," said Mama.

"And happier and funnier," giggled Ellen.

"And smarter and braver and swimmier," said Hildy.

"And *louder!*" boomed Jug.

And George barked *Rumpf!* to that.